touch blue

BY CYNTHIA LORD

Scholastic Inc.
New York   Toronto   London   Auckland
Sydney   Mexico City   New Delhi   Hong Kong

This book was originally published in hardcover
by Scholastic Press in 2010.

ISBN 978-0-545-03532-3

12 11 10 9 8 7 6 5 4 3 2 1   12 13 14 15 16 17/0

Printed in the U.S.A.   40   This edition first printing, June 2012

The display type was set in Ad Lib BT and Copperplate Regular.

The text type was set in Cochin Regular.

Book design by Marijka Kostiw

TO

MY PARENTS,

WHO TAUGHT ME

THE JOY

AND IMPORTANCE

OF FAMILY

ACKNOWLEDGMENTS

In this book about luck, it feels especially appropriate to admit I am the luckiest author on earth to work with such a gifted editor as Leslie Budnick. Thank you, Leslie, for sharing your genius with this book, and for all the grace, patience, humor, and warmth you've shown me on this book's journey.

My sincere thank-you to my wonderful agent, Tracey Adams, and to everyone at Scholastic, especially Marijka Kostiw, David Saylor, and Adam Rau, and to Anne Dunn for adding their remarkable talents to this book.

A special thanks to my critique groups and writing friends, who have read many drafts of this book and always encouraged me to keep going. A big hug to Terry Farish and Toni Buzzeo — it was a best-luck day for me when we became critique partners.

Grateful appreciation to Kaelyn and Clay Porter, Mark Wallace, Tori Arau, Mona Pease, and Kathleen Clemons, who let me ask lots of questions and patiently answered each one.

And finally, thank you to my family. I love you all.

A grant from the Society of Children's Book Writers and Illustrators helped make this novel possible.

ONE

**Touch blue and
your wish will come true.**

"The ferry's coming!" High on the cliffs, my five-year-old sister, Libby, jumps foot to foot. "Come on, Tess! Mom says we can run down to meet it!"

Across the bay the ferry looks small as a toy leaving the mainland wharf. I've seen that boat heading for our island hundreds of times, but never with my heart pounding so hard.

He's almost here!

"I hope Aaron likes to play Monopoly and swing at the playground," Libby calls down to me. "Do you think he will?"

"He's thirteen. That's probably too old for swinging." I know what Libby means, though. I want Aaron to like everything I do, too: reading, fishing, building things, riding bikes, and cannonballing off the ferry float into the ocean. Ever since my best friend, Amy Hamilton, and her family moved off the island last winter, I've missed having someone to do those things with. When you live on a small island, you don't get many choices of friends.

The wind quivers a brown strand of hair over my nose. My bangs are in that awful growing-out stage: too short to stay tucked behind my ears and too long to stay out of my eyes. As I wipe that hair away, I notice something sparkle near my feet among the tangles of rockweed. I reach down and pry loose a palm-sized circle of blue sea glass, just the bottom of a bottle. Once it was someone's trash, but now the ocean has tumbled it all smooth and beautiful.

It's extra lucky to find something blue, because there's a saying, *Touch blue and your wish will come true.* So anything blue comes with a wish attached.

Lifting the sea glass up to my eye, I watch the whole world change: The far and near islands, the lobster boats in the bay, the summer cottages ringing the shore, even Mrs. Ellis's tiny American and Maine flags flapping in the wind beside her wharf turn hazy, cobalt blue.

Across the water the fancy mainland houses with their big windows stare blank-eyed back at me. Funny to think we islanders are their "view." I stick out my tongue to give them something new to look at.

Tunneling my toes under the silty clam-flat mud, I imagine Dad standing at the ferryboat's rail, pointing out the islands to the boy beside him. I hope Dad doesn't show Aaron everything. Aaron's never lived on an island before, and I want to show him things, too. He's probably never seen a seal pop his head up in the water, almost near enough to touch. Or watched a thunderstorm over the ocean, with miles and miles of lightning strikes flashing at once. And I'm extra excited to show Aaron how close it feels to flying when Dad guns the engine of our lobster boat and it skims, fast as a skipping stone, over a flat sea.

"We do our best to make a good match," Natalie, Aaron's caseworker, had promised me when she came out to interview us.

I've never met a foster child before. But I've read books about them. There's Gilly in *The Great Gilly Hopkins*, Bud in *Bud, Not Buddy*, and Anne Shirley in *Anne of Green Gables*. I hope Aaron's the most like Anne: full of stories and eager to meet us. Of course, he won't be *exactly* like Anne, because he's not eleven years old.

Or a girl.

Or Canadian.

"Take it slow, Tess," Mom had said this morning over breakfast. "Remember what Natalie said? We

3

need to give Aaron some space. Don't overwhelm him with questions today."

"I won't ask questions," I promised. "I'll just *tell* him things."

Something hits my shoulder.

Up on the cliffs, Libby's hands are full of fat, Scotch-pine cones. She scowls at me and pitches another, but it falls short. "Let's go, Tess! We'll miss the ferry!"

I glance to the boat crossing the bay now. "All right. I'm coming!" Running over the clam flats, my feet slap the muck. Broken mussel shells jab my feet, and my toes clench from the cold water, but I run faster with each smacking step. It might be June, but it'll be weeks before the flats feel warm under my feet.

At the break in the cliffs, I drop the sea glass into my shorts pocket to free my hands for climbing. I know exactly where to place my feet, which rocks wiggle and which ones won't.

"Maybe Aaron'll like green beans!" Libby shouts down to me.

I grin up at her. "Why? So you can give him *yours*?" Stepping up to a flat ledge, I grab a little tree to steady myself. "Or maybe Aaron'll like boats and reading, like me!"

4

"Or maybe Aaron'll be able to whistle real good." Libby blows, but only a whoosh of air comes.

"You've almost got it."

Libby reaches her hands high overhead. "Or maybe he'll be a hundred feet tall!" Her short blond hair and green plastic barrettes bob as she giggles.

Laughing with her, I clamber up the last ledge and pick up my sneakers from the grass where I'd left them. "If Aaron were that big, he wouldn't fit in our house."

"Or on the ferry!" Libby adds.

I look over my shoulder at the boat — closer now! Straight on, the ferry looks like a fat birthday cake from this distance, wide at the bottom, the tall wheel-house rising like a candle in the middle.

I drop my sneakers and slide my feet into them, without even brushing the sand away.

"Hey!" Libby yells as I run past her. "Wait for me!"

But I am so full from waiting today that I can't swallow one more drop — not even for Libby. Reaching into my pocket, I touch that lucky-blue sea glass and try to cram all my wishes about Aaron into one.

Please let this plan work.

TWO

**A redhead on a boat
is unlucky.**

By the time Libby and I reach the ferry landing, the wharf's already crowded with tourists and islanders. I wave to Aunt Barb and Uncle Ned, but I ignore Eben Calder standing over by the rail with some summer kids. Stocky with more freckles (and less brains) than a slab of granite, Eben might be the youngest Calder, but he's mean as any — especially toward me. Ever since kindergarten, Eben's been a thorn in my side: always picking on me and trying to outdo me at everything.

"Do you see Aaron?" Libby presses her way up beside me.

On tiptoes, I steal a look between Reverend Beal's arm and Mrs. Coombs's shoulder. The ferry has pulled close enough that I can easily read the name *Island View* on the navy blue hull. I recognize some of the passengers standing in the bow and sitting on the red benches of the upper deck, but I don't see Dad.

"Not yet," I tell Libby. "They must be inside on the main deck." As the crew ties up, I chew my thumbnail to keep my hands busy and listen to scraps of conversation around me:

"Of course, it's bound to change some things. . . ."

". . . five kids in all — the same number we lost when the Hamiltons moved away."

". . . had to come up with some way to save the school, didn't we? And the State would only give us the summer to work it out."

I turn my head, just enough to see the Hamiltons' old house down the shore. If wishes worked backward, I would've wished on that piece of lucky-blue sea glass that Amy and her family hadn't moved off the island last winter. If they hadn't left, the State of Maine wouldn't be threatening to shut down our small island school, saying we don't have enough kids to keep it open now. Plus I would still have my best friend.

If our school closes, Mom'll lose her job as the island teacher, and many of the families living here with kids — including us — will have to move to the mainland to go to school. The mainland may not be far away in miles, but those miles change everything.

"We can't leave here!" I told Dad. "I don't want to

go to a new school where I don't know anyone — where all the other kids have made their friends already!"

But he said our family needs Mom's income and the health insurance that comes with her job. "I don't see a way around it, Tess," he said, spreading his hands.

Until one February night when Reverend Beal came to our house with a plan. "It'll solve everything," he said. "We'll have the same number of students we had before the Hamiltons moved, and we'll give some needy children good homes. As I see it, this could be a good thing all around. The Rosses have already said yes, and the Morrells have agreed to take *two* kids. The Webbers are thinking about it."

Sitting at the kitchen table, I waited for Dad to say it was a crazy idea for our family to take in a foster child to help get our school numbers up again. But he just sat there, stroking his beard between his thumb and fingers.

"The older children are harder to place, and the caseworker seemed very pleased that we might be willing to take a teenager, as well as the younger ones," Reverend Beal continued. "If we get going now, we might have this all settled by summer, well before school starts in the fall."

I held my breath and let myself imagine it: Mom not worried about her job anymore and Dad not talking about selling our house, and me staying right here with everything I know and love. I'm sure Mom and Dad would take great care of that kid, too. So maybe it could be a good thing all around?

"I don't know," Dad said. "It doesn't seem completely *right*."

"We have a strong, loving home." Mom's index finger circled the top of her coffee mug, the way it does when she's trying to talk Dad into something. "How can it be wrong to share that with a child who needs one — even if he brings us something in return?"

Dad couldn't answer that, so today a thirteen-year-old boy is moving into our attic.

Libby's just learning to add, so I explained Aaron's life mathematically to her by drawing it in the wet sand with a stick one day:

5 + 6 + 1 + 1 = 13

Aaron had lived with his mother until he was five years old. Then some people from the State took him away, because they thought his mom wasn't doing a good enough job of taking care of him. Next he'd lived with his grandma for six years, until she died.

And after that, he'd lived one year each in two foster homes.

"Why didn't he go back to his mom when his grandma died?" Libby asked.

"He couldn't." I took a deep breath, wondering how to explain the situation in words she'd understand. "No one knew where Aaron's mom was when his grandma died. She didn't show up to the meetings she was supposed to go to, and now Aaron doesn't belong to her anymore. A judge said so."

"Could a judge say that about *me*?" Libby asked, her eyes wide.

"No. Don't worry," I told her. "We're fine. But Aaron needs a new family now, and that's gonna be us."

As the ferry crew slides the ramp into position, I wonder what Aaron's thinking. Is he scared, hoping we'll like him? I practice my biggest smile, so he'll feel welcome immediately.

"Hey, Tess!" a familiar voice says.

I tip my chin up to use all my height. Even though I'm eleven years old and Jenna Ross is only ten, I always feel short and plain standing next to her. Jenna's already half a head taller than me, and she has golden curls, like the angel in the stained-glass window at church. My hair's pitch brown and straight as pine needles.

I suspect Jenna would like to be my best friend now that Amy is gone, but it feels doubly wrong. Not only because Jenna can't ever replace Amy, but also because Amy never liked Jenna. She said Jenna was stuck-up over being pretty.

"I hope the new kids are nice," Jenna says. "Especially Aaron and Grace."

The other island foster families wanted kids close to Libby's age, but I'm happy we're getting an older one. Aaron'll be able to do more things with me. And I think it'll be fun to be a little sister for a change, instead of always being the responsible older kid.

"I baked Grace a cake to celebrate her first day with us," Jenna says. "I hope she likes chocolate."

Why didn't I think of that? I should've made Aaron something.

"Does Aaron have to go to meetings with his real parents?" Jenna whispers. "We'll have to take Grace to the mainland every Tuesday, because her mom's trying to get her back eventually."

I shake my head. "Aaron doesn't belong to his mother anymore — not legally, anyway."

"I wish it were like that for us. It feels like we only get to borrow Grace." Jenna sighs. "We even have to get permission for her to have a haircut."

"Why can't *Grace* decide?" I ask. "It's her hair."

Before Jenna can answer, someone shouts, "Here they come!" and we both jump to our tiptoes.

"Can you see Aaron *now*?" Libby steps on my foot to make herself taller.

"Ouch! Get off me, Lib." My eyes skim the line of passengers hurrying off the main deck. A tourist wearing a huge backpack steps gingerly from the ferry ramp to the wooden float, holding up the line behind her.

"Go!" I whisper, wanting her out of the way.

I see Mr. Webber bend down to tie a little boy's sneaker. Beside them, Mrs. Ross smiles, patting the long blond hair of a little girl clutching a stuffed panda and a picture book.

"That's Grace!" Jenna weaves a path through the crowd.

On the metal gangplank, the passengers' footsteps boom like a thunderstorm. A wet breeze off the water raises goose bumps on my skin, and I rub my arms to warm them. The air smells, a mix of salt water, bait, pine trees, wet wood, and diesel fuel.

A few tourists grab the rail as the ramp rolls back and forth with each ocean wave. Behind them, some islanders pull coolers on wheels and carry extra-large tote bags crammed full of groceries. Glancing back to the ferry, I spy Dad's Red Sox cap in the line of passengers. "There they are!" I wave, but Dad's speaking to the ferry crew, who are unloading boxes, groceries, and bags of mail.

Then I see Aaron. Skinny as a spar, he seems too tall for thirteen, with a pinched-sour mouth and red hair. A redhead on a boat is unlucky! Why didn't I remember to mention *that* to his caseworker? His hair, bright as October leaves, falls near to his shoulders.

"Does he look like someone who'll love swinging?" Libby asks, straining to see.

People push around me, but I can't move. I don't know what I was expecting, but I wasn't expecting Aaron to be *this* boy. He looks weak, with skin so white it seems almost unreal. He'll burn to a crisp out fishing with us.

He can't help those things, but still—

In front of me, Mrs. Coombs tsks her tongue. "That redheaded one's a juvenile delinquent if ever I saw one."

"Now, Shirley." Reverend Beal starts in preaching about Jesus, but I can only stare at the boy climbing the gangplank. Aaron never once touches the rail — just clutches a black musical instrument case in one hand and keeps the other pushed deep into a pocket of his leather jacket.

"This is Libby and Tess." Dad holds an old tan suitcase in one hand. "We're all glad you're here, Aaron. Isn't that right, girls?"

"Yes!" Libby shoves by me and throws her arms around Aaron's waist.

Aaron lifts one hand cautiously. He gives Libby a little, quick pat on her back and then steps away from her.

I push my lips into my widest, welcomest smile. "Hi, Aaron!"

He glances at me. His eyes are muddy green, like the sea deep in the coves. "Hi." He says it flatly, like I'm just anybody.

Why'd Natalie pick this boy for us? A fear whispers in me that maybe she didn't have anywhere else to send him.

Walking down the wharf, I hear Dad stumble a few words about the island and how living here might take some getting used to, but it's a good place.

We pass the ferry landing parking lot full of old or second-best island vehicles: station wagons with

1970s wood paneling, golf carts, motorcycles, motor-ized scooters, and every kind of beat-up truck you can name.

"When you live on an island, you need two cars," Dad explains. "The newer one stays on the mainland, and the older one comes to the island — to die." He gives a joking smile.

But when Dad looks away, Aaron rolls his eyes.

I reach into my pocket to touch that blue sea glass. Maybe I should've been more specific with my wish?

THREE

**Start your journey with your right foot
and good luck will walk with you.**

As we walk home, the narrow island road crackles under our feet, speckled purple and blue from the mussel shells the seagulls have dropped on the tar to break them open. Libby skips ahead of us, pointing out things to Aaron — except she's showing him things no one needs to be told about. "These are white birch trees, and here are some telephone poles. This is the golf course. And we have swings up at the playground!"

"And there's a basketball court and tennis courts outside the Community Center," I say over Libby's voice. It's the only way I can get a word in. "They have equipment you can borrow. Not you *specifically*," I say quickly, in case that sounds like I was offering him charity. Mom had said to be careful not to make Aaron feel embarrassed if he didn't have something. "Anyone can borrow racquets and nets from there. You just have to sign them out."

Aaron doesn't say a word.

I sigh. I'm trying to look on the bright side here. Even though Aaron isn't the kid I would've picked, Anne of Green Gables wasn't what her new family expected either, and that worked out fine.

"And that's the MacCreadys' dog!" Libby continues. "Her name is Roxie."

Lots of people are outside today, raking leftover leaves off their gardens or working on their fishing gear — painting buoys or repairing traps.

"Hello, Jacob!" old Mrs. Ellis calls to us, watering the window boxes on her front porch. "Is that your foster boy?"

I cringe. "Foster boy" sounds rude, even if it's right.

Dad squeezes Aaron's shoulder, then murmurs from the corner of his mouth, "Don't mind her."

"This is Aaron!" I yell.

As we walk, Aaron twists just enough to lose Dad's hand off his shoulder. At the next house, Karen Moody pulls her cell phone from her ear and waves. "Welcome to Bethsaida, Aaron!"

And at Phipps's Gas and Groceries, Ben Phipps leans out the window by the cash register. "Hey, I see your boy's here, Jacob!"

With each new person who calls to us, Aaron's nod looks more forced and his chest droops a little lower. "How come all these people already know about me?" he asks, wary.

"Islands are like this," Dad says. "You'll get used to it."

Living on an island does have its share of good-luck/bad-luck parts. One good/bad thing is how everyone knows everyone else. That's good luck if you need a stick of butter or help launching your boat. The bad luck is that it's near impossible to keep a secret on Bethsaida, because everyone knows everyone else's business.

"You really can only leave here by boat?" Aaron asks. "There's no other way to get off the island?"

I follow his worried gaze past the familiar mailboxes and dirt driveways of a few summer cottages to the waves glimmering with late-afternoon sunlight.

"You can't *drive* to the mainland!" Libby giggles, skipping along. "You'd fall off the island! Right, Dad? Kerplunk! Smack in the ocean!"

Willie Buston's pickup truck speeds toward us along the road. Going that fast, he must be trying to make the ferry. Willie waves as he passes, but Aaron jumps — right into the blueberry bushes on the roadside.

I bite my lip to keep from grinning. Just then, Eben Calder swerves around us on his bicycle — showing off by cutting it close, even though he's got plenty of room.

I suppose that's another good-luck/bad-luck thing about Bethsaida: There are only a few roads (and no speed limits or sidewalks). On the good-luck side, you can't get lost. But on the bad-luck side, living on a scrap of land only a handful of miles wide by another handful long means it's harder to get away from the people who annoy you. Not only do I have to see Eben Calder at school, on the ferry, at the store, in church, and swerving his bike around me on the road, but the Calders' house is right next to the shack where Dad and I get our lobster bait every morning.

Mom says I should be kind to Eben, because he doesn't get a lot of attention from his mom and dad. I don't see why that means I have to be nice all the time and he gets to be a jerk, though.

"Afternoon, Margery," Dad says. I hadn't noticed Margery Poule kneeling in the garden behind her picket fence.

"Hello, Jacob!" She waves her trowel. "And this must be Aaron?"

"Aaron's my new brother!" Libby announces, making

him flinch. "Except his last name is Spinney, not Brooks."

"How nice!" Mrs. Poule points her trowel at the case in Aaron's hand. "What instrument do you play, dear?"

"Trumpet and piano," he says.

"And he's not a hundred feet tall!" Libby continues. "But we don't know yet if he likes green beans or if he can whistle or play Monopoly." She plants her hands on her hips. "Or read!"

Dad holds up his palm to stop her. "That's enough, Lib. No need to find out everything in the first half hour."

As we walk, Libby skips ahead so she can be first to tell Mom we're here. I match my step to Aaron's. "Sometimes we have island concerts and sing-alongs."

Was that a flicker of interest on his face? "And there's a talent show every August. Some people play instruments in the show."

"I don't like to play for other people."

He says it plainly, but it still feels like a snub.

"We also have a library," I say, trying again. "It's probably not as big as you're used to on the mainland, but our librarian can get any book you want from another library, as long as you're not in a hurry."

"I don't read much."

"Well, what *do* you like to — ?" I start, but one look at Dad's lowered eyebrows shuts my mouth. Oh, yeah. I'm not supposed to ask a bunch of questions. But talking to Aaron is like trying to start a campfire with a box of wet matches — it's near impossible to get anything going.

I try to remember everything it said on that checklist Mom and Dad got at foster-parent class: "Your First Days at Home with Your Foster Child" had hung on our refrigerator for the past month and suddenly disappeared this morning. Mom probably didn't want Aaron to know we were new to this whole thing and needed a list to tell us what to do.

But in all those dos and don'ts about setting up a bedroom, feeding the kid as soon as he arrives in case he hadn't eaten all day, explaining house rules, giving the child some chores so he'll feel part of the family faster, and being ready for the new kid to feel sad about leaving his last place behind, it didn't mention how weird it might feel for us, too.

"Here's our house," Dad says as we turn into our driveway.

Mom is waiting on the porch. "Hi, Aaron! We're so excited to meet you. Supper's about ready, so come right in."

"I wanted hamburgers tonight," Libby says to Aaron. "But Mom said you probably didn't get to eat ocean stuff all the time like we do. And she told me I have to knock to come visit you in your room. So listen for me, okay?"

Aaron looks at our three-storied house, gray with green shutters and built tall enough for the attic window to look out over the treetops to the ocean. I watch his gaze slide past the stack of wire lobster traps waiting to be repaired next to the shed, to our clothesline hung with newly painted buoys, gleaming with Dad's colors: navy blue with yellow stripes.

"It's quicker to hang lobster buoys up when you paint them," I explain. "That way you can paint and dry them all the way around. Each lobsterman paints his own colors and pattern on his buoys, so he'll know which traps belong to him."

Then I follow Aaron's eyes beyond the clothesline to my new pride and joy: an old wooden skiff, resting on sawhorses. Upside down, the hull is sun-faded white and rounded, like the belly of a porpoise. I have to remove several layers of old paint, but once she's scraped down smooth and painted over, she'll look good as new.

"I'll live here?" Aaron asks quietly.

The little catch in his voice makes me turn. I don't know if he's even expecting an answer, but I nod anyway.

"Welcome home," I say.

F O U R

If you watch a boat disappear from view,
you'll never see it again.

The first night, Aaron asks to go to bed early, even though we had rented a family movie and I made popcorn. We watch the movie without him, but it doesn't feel right — like having a birthday party without the guest of honor.

"It's been a long day for him," Mom says, collecting our popcorn bowls after the movie. "Aaron probably just wanted a little time by himself to unpack and get used to things."

"Tess, maybe you could show Aaron the island in the morning?" Dad adds, turning off the TV. "And introduce him around?"

"Sure," I say. "I already know lots of places to show him."

"Can I come, too?" Libby asks. *"Please?"*

"Not this time," Mom says.

Libby pouts. "If Tess gets to take Aaron somewhere all by herself, I want a turn with just me and him, too!"

As Mom takes Libby upstairs to bed, I follow Dad into the kitchen. "Dad?" I lower my voice, even though no one's close enough to listen. "What'll happen if Aaron doesn't want to stay with us? Can he ask Natalie to move him?"

"Have you given up already?" he asks, pouring water into the coffeemaker for morning.

"No, but he doesn't seem to like it here. What if this doesn't work out?"

Dad shrugs. "I don't know for sure, but I suspect if he's miserable, Natalie might try to move him somewhere else. Island living isn't for everyone."

"If that happens, can we get another kid before the summer's over?"

Dad frowns, spooning coffee into the filter. "No. We're not gonna keep borrowing other people's children just so we don't have to leave this place."

"But—"

"No buts." He lets the top of the coffeemaker slam closed. "Moving isn't the worst thing that can happen to a person, Tess."

I back slowly out of the kitchen, letting him think he got the last word. But in my head I answer, *Yes, it is.*

In the morning, I take Aaron to my favorite places on the island, hoping to find one he'll like.

At Chandler's Cove, I lead the way, climbing over huge pieces of driftwood, bleached white as bones. Aaron walks around them.

From the top of Strout's Hill, I show him how far you can see up and down the bay. It's a beautiful morning, the waves glittering with sun. I point out the lighthouse and two sailboats, pale as tissue paper, racing out to sea. "Do you see how the sparkles get thicker and closer together the farther out you look? Doesn't it look like those sailboats are sledding on snow? But don't keep looking, because if you watch a boat until it's out of sight, you'll never see it again." I turn away before the boats disappear from view, but I don't need to worry, because Aaron's checking his watch.

"When does your family eat lunch?" he asks.

"Noontime, but we could stop at the store and get a snack. Come on!"

As we head back to the main road, I introduce Aaron to everyone I know, even the summer people, like Mrs. Palozzi, who is painting her front steps gray.

"Nice to meet you, Aaron," she says.

He kicks a little rock at his feet. "Hi."

"Did you have a good winter, Tess?" Mrs. Palozzi asks. "It's so nice to be back here. Though I can't believe how noisy the birds were this morning. Did you hear them? I had to get out of bed at five o'clock to close my windows!"

Some summer people get called "summer complaints" by the islanders because they come to Bethsaida to get away from their winter lives, then spend the whole summer complaining that the island's not more like the place they left behind.

Painted birthday-cake colors, the line of summer cottages looks like a row of life-sized dollhouses. All winter they sit empty, but the Palozzis are back now in the yellow house, and a shiny new barbeque grill sits beside the pink one. It's easy to tell which houses are year-round on Bethsaida and which aren't. Summer people never have any broken-down things in their yards.

"After Labor Day, you can cut across those lawns," I explain to Aaron as we walk, "but the gray house down at the end is Mrs. Coombs's house. Don't ever shortcut across her grass, because she lives here all year, and she'll call Mom."

Mrs. Coombs is a *year-round* complaint.

"And on the other side of her house is the parish hall." I point to the white building with its little belfry rising from the roof peak. "It's an old schoolhouse from a long time ago when the island had so many kids it needed two schools. But now it's where we have bean suppers, Lobstering Association meetings, and special events like the summer talent show and the Christmas party."

Amy and I always did a funny skit together for the talent show — last year we did a fake newscast, *Live from Bethsaida*. Amy was the anchorwoman, Tori Sparkleteeth. She sat behind a desk and pretended to read from a stack of papers. She'd say, all serious, "There was some screaming heard at Phipps's Gas and Groceries today. Let's go now to Tess, live on the scene!" Then I would pick someone to interview from the audience. No one knew ahead of time I would be interviewing them. I'd ask questions like "Where were you when the screams came?" and "Can you demonstrate what it sounded like?" Our newscast was a big hit at the talent show. In fact, Amy and I probably would've done it again if she hadn't moved.

Mom thinks I should do something with Libby this year, but Libby's only idea so far is that we dress up like puppies and let people pet us.

And there's no way I'm getting up there alone. I'll just *watch* the show this year.

"Here's our school." I gesture to the small, one-story red building. "There are four rooms in the school building — two on each side of the main door. The two front rooms are classrooms, and then there's a kitchen where we eat lunch, and a little office with a bathroom. But all the kids only have one teacher — and that's Mom. She's a good teacher. You'll like her, even though you can't ever say 'I don't have any homework' if you really do, because she knows."

Some mainland kids would probably hate going to a little island school, but I love it. For me, it sounds like a nightmare to be in a huge building with all those hallways and hundreds of kids, where there are a bazillion buses and you don't know where to go and don't know people's names. I wouldn't have anyone to eat lunch with — or even know how to get lunch at a big cafeteria. And what if I couldn't find my classes?

"I'll be in the same class with *kindergartners*?" Aaron wrinkles his nose.

"You won't do the same *work* as them. You'll have a folder, and you'll work on your own schoolwork while Mom works with other grades. Then she'll call you up when it's your turn. You'll do a lesson with her and maybe a couple other kids, if they have the same lesson as you."

Aaron shakes his head. "I can't believe I had to quit my jazz band to come here."

It's on the tip of my tongue to say, "You would've had to leave it anyway." Aaron's previous foster mom didn't want to do foster care anymore, and that's why he was available for us.

As we turn the corner, I see Jenna and Grace riding bicycles. "We're going to see Libby!" Jenna yells as they pass us.

Grace grins, pedaling hard to keep up. How come Jenna gets it so easy? Grace looks happy to be with her — like Jenna doesn't even have to try.

"Do you know Grace?" I ask Aaron.

He shakes his head. "Why would I know her?"

I open my mouth to say, "Because you're both foster kids," but stop myself just in time. "Um, you came on the ferry together. Look, here's the store!" I say quickly, shifting the subject. "Let's go in and get something to eat."

As Aaron and I cross the porch at Phipps's Gas and Groceries, I wave to the Morrell family in their beat-up station wagon driving by. Their two new foster children are twin brothers, Henry and Matthew. One of the boys is looking curiously out the backseat window. I give him an even bigger wave, and he smiles. I bet the Morrells are showing their new kids around the island, too.

Reverend Beal thought maybe we should have a party to welcome the new kids to Bethsaida, but Natalie said no. She said it might make them feel different from everyone else. "Just getting used to a new family and a new home is enough."

Walking across the store porch, I love the hollow thud of my footsteps on the wood — it sounds like I'm walking on a wharf. I scan the bulletin board above the newspaper machine and a row of empty milk crates. The Ladies' Aid Society wants clean things in good condition for their rummage sale. There's a knitting group forming at the library. And there are plenty of new index-card announcements from islanders advertising caretaking, gardening, and carpentry services for the summer people.

I open the white screen door. Ben Phipps is behind the cash register, Karen Moody is buying milk, and behind her in line, Lee Fowler is holding a loaf of bread. "This is Aaron," I announce. As they're all saying "Hi" and "Nice to meet you," I take a couple of whoopie pies off the plate on the counter and a bottle of my favorite orange soda from the cooler.

I hold the cooler door open for Aaron, but he hesitates. "It's okay. Mom gave me enough money for both of us."

Aaron chooses a half-sized can of cola—the smallest they sell. "I'm not really hungry."

When Ben Phipps rings me up, he nods toward the store's lobster tank. "Tell your father to catch me some good-sized lobsters, Tess. The tourists are starting to come in."

I nod. "I'll tell him."

For someone who said he's not hungry, Aaron eats his whoopie pie plenty fast—before we're even off the store steps. I take my time with mine, holding it sideways so I can stick my tongue into the white, sugary filling between the two round chocolate cake halves.

Outside, at one of the outdoor picnic tables, an old man's reading the newspaper. I smirk to myself at his checked shirt, plaid shorts, and black socks. "That tourist must be running low on laundry," I whisper to Aaron.

He doesn't smile, and I wonder if it's because Aaron didn't come with a lot of clothes either.

"Bye," I say to the old man.

"You take care," he replies, barely looking up from his paper.

When we're away from the store, Aaron turns to me. "Do we have to wave or talk to *everyone*?"

"People are friendly," I say. "What's wrong with that?"

"I hate people staring at me. And how can anyone think when you get interrupted all the time?"

Nothing pleases this boy!

We pass the church and the parsonage, two white buildings separated by a parking lot and a red petunia border, but I close my mouth and don't point them out. Though I suppose the sharp steeple, arched doors, and stained-glass windows are a dead giveaway. The side rear door to the church is propped open. Swells of organ music float out from inside.

Aaron pauses.

"Do you need to rest?" I ask. "I thought walking would show you more of the island, but maybe bikes would've been a better idea — oh, and we have extra bikes at our house. So one can be yours."

Aaron's head moves ever so slightly with the beat of the music. His mouth is partly open, his eyes on the side of the church.

"Mrs. Ellis must be practicing for Sunday," I say. "She keeps threatening to quit. She says the alto section of the choir is getting too big for themselves, wanting new hymnals when the old ones have done fine since forever. Wait! Didn't you say you play the piano? Maybe —"

"Can't you shut up for one minute?"

I stare at the side of his face, as shocked as if he'd suddenly turned and bit me. In the pause between the hymn's verses, I hear the soft whoosh of the wind moving through the trees, a few chirping insects and birds. Then the organ rises up again. Stern as thunder, the bass notes boom so low I feel them in my toes.

Standing on the road beside Aaron, I don't tell him he hurt my feelings. I don't ask why he doesn't try even a little. I don't point out that he has to live *somewhere*, and at least we want him. And I don't admit the thing I'm most scared of.

We've all made a big mistake.

FIVE

Cross your fingers
for good luck.

Aaron and I barely even look at each other as we walk home together on the wooded road that runs down the center of the island. My flip-flops slap the road, sounding extra loud in the quiet between us.

Near the shore, Bethsaida is a busy place. The houses sit close together, people are often outside, and things are going on — especially in the summer. But once you lose sight of the water, the island is mostly forest and the buildings are far apart. On the inner roads, you can even forget you're on an island.

But that feeling doesn't last. A few miles forward or back, and there's the water again. Because no matter which route you choose, every road on Bethsaida ends at the ocean.

Aaron kicks a rock. It bounces along the cracked and patched-up tar. "What do you *do* out here?"

The flatness in his voice prickles me, like he's already decided the answer to his question. "Plenty of things! Besides all the stuff I've already *told* you, there are picnics. Clubs. Basketball games. Movie nights." I pause, because even to me that doesn't sound like a lot. "And I'm fixing up my own boat."

If I said that to an island boy, he'd say, "Oooh," but Aaron just stares at the cat-o'-nine-tails growing in the swampy ditch near the post office.

"Come on," I mutter. "I need to get the mail." I want to see if Amy sent me a letter. I promised myself I wouldn't write any more letters to Amy until she wrote to me again, but I miss her. Summer isn't much fun without her. And Amy was the one person I could tell anything to, and now it feels like all my worries are stacking up inside me. What if this doesn't work out with Aaron? What if we've gone to all this trouble of bringing him here but he hates it so much he begs Natalie to move him? It'll be extra bad if this whole plan fails because of *our* family.

Or what if Aaron runs away? That's what Bud did in *Bud, Not Buddy* when he got sent to a foster home he hated. Of course, it's not really the same. Bud's foster brother was so mean that he stuck a pencil up Bud's nose while he was asleep. I was so nice that I made popcorn for Aaron — even if he didn't eat it.

When I push open the door, the postmaster looks over his half-moon glasses at Aaron, then at me. "Hi, you two."

"Mr. Moody, this is Aaron." I glance over my shoulder.

"Where are you from, Aaron?" Mr. Moody asks.

Aaron hesitates. I watch his Adam's apple roll as he swallows. "You mean *right* before here?"

Mr. Moody looks embarrassed. "Oh, yes. I didn't mean to —"

"He lived in Rangeley," I add quickly. "Before here."

"Rangeley? I was up there fishing two years ago," Mr. Moody says. "We rented a cabin from some very nice people. Let's see, what was their name?"

I cross my fingers for good luck before I open our mailbox. *Let there be a letter today.* I pull out the stack of mail and flip quickly through bills, advertisements, and an oversized envelope. Glancing at the return address, I see STATE OF MAINE at the top.

Oh! My breath catches in my throat. I know I shouldn't open mail addressed to Mom and Dad, but this must be the State's official answer about our school staying open or closing. And that affects me, too.

I pause only a second before ripping open the envelope.

"What was the name of the person you lived with in Rangeley?" Mr. Moody asks, behind me.

"Mrs. Armstrong," Aaron says.

Hands shaking, I reach in the envelope for the letter. But I'm surprised to find a smaller envelope inside: a lemon yellow one, addressed to Aaron.

For Aaron? My whole body slumps with disappointment. I suppose I ought to have guessed the State could be sending my parents mail about Aaron now, too. But I thought for sure it was about the school.

I should've wished for a letter for *me.* Up in the left-hand corner of the yellow envelope, it says "C. Spinney" with an address in Connecticut. A purple Post-it note stuck to the front says: *Hi, Mrs. Brooks, This letter is from Aaron's mom. I checked his file, and it says he can receive mail from her. So when you think he's ready for it, go ahead and give it to him. Sincerely, Emily (Natalie's assistant)*

Today feels like one giant snowball of bad luck, getting fatter with every turn. First, Aaron doesn't like anything about being here. Then I didn't get a letter from Amy or an answer about the school. Now

Aaron's mom writes to him — like she's claiming him, before we even get to know him! And when I get home, I'm gonna have to admit I opened Dad and Mom's mail, and —

"Will you tell her, Tess?" Mr. Moody asks.

I startle. Aaron has come up beside me — I didn't even hear him coming! Mr. Moody looks at me from behind the counter, but Aaron gasps, staring at the envelope in my hands.

Oh, glory. "What?"

Mr. Moody smiles. "I asked you to tell your mother I delivered some packages to the school this morning. I left them inside the door. Looked to me like school supplies or maybe books."

"Oh, um, yeah. I'll tell her." I slam our tiny mailbox shut and spin the combination lock. "Come on, Aaron."

When we're outside, he makes a grab for the yellow envelope. I let him take it — it's his letter. As he's ripping open the envelope, I take a step closer.

. . . miss you so much. They took you from me — I never wanted it to happen. I think about you all the time and some nights I can't stop crying, wondering where you are and if those people are being good to you.

What does she mean, "those people"? I move a little more. Aaron's thumb's in the way. His fingers are graceful-looking, long and smooth. Not like mine, roughed by salt water and calloused from handling rope and gear.

I bet you've grown so much I'd hardly recognize you. I'm doing better now. I'm trying to —

"Do you mind?" Aaron shields the letter with his hand.

I pretend I was looking around me, not reading over his arm. "I'm sorry. Is your mom okay?"

"She only just found out my grandma died," he says, turning the page to read the back. "I tried to tell her when it happened, but no one knew where she was."

I sigh. "My best friend, Amy, promised she'd write to me when she moved away last winter. I've sent her six letters and three e-mails, and she's only sent me two letters back."

Why'd I tell him that? I blush. It sounds so small compared to his problems. But still, I don't think I can stand him being mean about it.

He nods, though. "Don't tell anyone about my letter, okay? I don't want my mom to get in trouble. Natalie probably won't like some of the things Mom says in here."

I run my tongue over my bottom lip. I don't like keeping things from my parents. But I also don't want anyone to get in trouble (including me for opening mail that wasn't mine).

"Please?" he asks. "It's been four years since I've heard from her. If Natalie gets mad at her, my mom might not write to me again."

"Won't Natalie ask about it?"

He shrugs. "Probably not. But if she does, your parents'll say they never got a letter. That'll be the truth."

I sigh. Natalie's assistant did say he could have the letter. So I'm only speeding up the "*go ahead and give it to him*" part. And I'd be sharing a secret with Aaron — at least that's sharing something.

"Okay," I say.

"Thanks." As he's folding the letter, I see Eben Calder riding his bike up the road with a Phipps's grocery bag under his arm.

"Hey, Mess!" he calls. "How's your orphan?"

"I'm not an orphan," Aaron says icily.

I take hold of Aaron's sleeve with one hand to hurry him along. With my other hand, I clutch the rest of our mail so tight that the advertisements crinkle. "Come on. Don't pay any attention to him."

I'm relieved when Eben passes us on the post office driveway. "Our island's only using you, Aaron," he

says over his shoulder. "Once we get those school numbers up, we'll be shipping all you kids off again."

"That's not true!" I say.

"What did you do to get sent to foster care?" Eben
asks. "Must've been something really bad if your own
mother didn't want you."

I spin around, ready to scream a whole stream of
ugly things at Eben. But Aaron has already wrenched
out of my grip and is charging down the post office
driveway, right toward Eben Calder getting off his
bike — and punches him smack in the face!

I don't know who's more surprised: me or Eben or
Mr. Moody, who's just coming out of the post office.
Aaron sends Eben reeling sideways, shoulder first into
a thicket of sea roses growing beside the steps.

Aaron takes off running. "Wait!" I yell, but he's fast.

"Why do you have to ruin everything?" I scream
at Eben.

By the time I reach the twist in the road, Aaron's
gone. All the way home, I alternate between feeling
terrible that Eben hurt Aaron's feelings and biting
back a tiny smile at how funny Eben looked with
his feet in the air, his bike wheel sticking upward,
still spinning.

"Mom?" I practice as I walk. "Something happened

today." She won't be happy that I let Aaron get in a fight and lost him — all on his first full day with us.

As I turn into our driveway, my neighbor calls from her porch swing, "What's the hurry, Tess?" Mrs. Varney'll talk forever, so I pretend I didn't hear her and race up our porch steps.

"Mom, something happen —"

But she's not in the kitchen. I open the door to the living room, but she's not there either.

"Mom?" I call up the stairs. Through the open window, I see Libby, Grace, and Jenna outside, sitting at our picnic table playing Monopoly, colorful piles of paper money all around them, each pile held down with a small rock against the breeze. Libby's wearing one of my sweaters, with the sleeves pushed up past her elbows.

Taking a few calming breaths to slow my heartbeat, I cross back to the kitchen. I'd better get my version in there quick, before Dad hears about the post office incident from someone else. I flip on the VHF radio on the counter, our link with Dad's lobster boat.

"Punched him right in the face!" a voice on the radio says.

I sigh. Too late.

"Ayuh, your boy knocked Eben right into a bunch of sea roses," another fisherman says. "Moody said it was quite a sight! Eben was hopping around like a jackrabbit, picking thorns out."

As I click off the radio, a trumpet note comes from somewhere above me. I would've expected a trumpet to sound hard-edged and piercing, but Aaron plays a scale fast and smooth, like a ball being tossed in the air, hovering at the tippy top before falling back to earth.

Climbing the stairs, I hold my breath, listening. I want to tell him I'm sorry about what happened. But even though I knock six times, he doesn't stop playing. So I open the door and go up the narrow attic stairway. Our attic has two rooms, separated by a half wall. The back side holds trunks, piled-up chairs, paintings stacked up under the eaves, and jumbled old things. The other side is Aaron's room now.

He's standing with his back to me in front of the attic's single, diamond-shaped window. Bordered by stained-glass rectangles — spruce green, bright blue, and thunderstorm gray — that window has the longest view in our whole house. Beyond the treetops, the sea sparkles, summer calm and postcard pretty.

"Aaron?"

He spins around, his trumpet against his bottom lip. "Don't you know how to knock?"

I feel the blood draining from my cheeks. "I did knock, but you were playing so loud you didn't hear me."

He doesn't have much stuff. He hasn't hung a single thing on the walls, and on his bureau is only a collage of photographs in a frame. Beside him is a skinny metal music stand with some sheet music stacked in the tray. The notes are jumping all over the place, like a bunch of paint splatters. His trumpet case is lying open on the new red comforter Mom bought him, and I see the corner of Aaron's old tan suitcase peeking out from under his bed.

Framed in the light from the window, Aaron seems only shadow.

"Eben Calder's a jerk," I say. "Don't listen to him, okay?"

"Was he telling the truth? Am I only here to keep your school open?"

I open my mouth to deny it, but he's bound to hear it sooner or later. "It's one reason. But we really wanted you, too."

He turns away from me, but not before I see him shake his head.

As I walk down the attic stairs, I pause a few times, hoping he'll say something. But he doesn't, and I close his door behind me.

Back in my room, I stare up at the ceiling. I hear his footsteps above me, pacing.

When he stops, the silence is as lonely as one bird calling.

SIX

Never

whistle on a boat.

The next morning I shut off my alarm at my usual four A.M. Though the room's still dark, I snatch my jeans off my bedroom floor and pull a bandanna, T-shirt, and hooded sweatshirt out of my bureau and dress as fast as I can.

Opening my sock drawer, I scoop my lucky things out of the corner, where I left them last night. Dad says a fisherman without his luck might as well stay ashore. So I always wear pants with pockets when I go fishing. That way I can bring my luck with me.

Two pennies from the year I was born.

A teeny plastic lobster, so I'll never come ashore without *any*.

A white quartz heart Amy gave me last Christmas.

My new circle of blue sea glass.

And finally, a quarter-sized shard of pottery that washed up on our beach. White on one side, the other has a blue outline of a sloop sailing on some waves. A long time ago, it was probably part of a whole scene painted on a fancy plate. One day when I was little, Dad and I were walking the shore and he stopped to pick it up. "Here's your first boat," he joked when he handed it to me.

I move my fingers over the objects in my pocket and say what I always say: "Bring me good luck."

Mom likes to say, "You make your *own* luck," but I don't think it's that simple. I believe good luck *does* float out there in the world, sticking fast to some people and leaving others behind. How else can you explain why some lobstermen — like Dad and Uncle Ned — always seem to know where the best "hot spots" are, while others barely catch enough to cover their costs? Or how I've lived in the same house with my own parents my whole life, and Aaron has lived in a string of places and has next to nothing of his own?

So when Mom says, "You make your own luck," I think, *Why take chances?* Especially when it's so easy to let the universe know what you want by touching blue or turning around three times or crossing your fingers.

I thought Aaron'd feel his bad luck had changed to have a real home with us, but he seems to feel unlucky to be here. Today, Dad and I are taking Aaron lobstering, though. My fingers are crossed that he'll like that.

Hurrying along the upstairs hallway, I pass my parents' bedroom and peek in to see Mom still sleeping, her brown braid trailing off the side of the bed. Last night I heard her arguing with Dad through my bedroom wall about whether or not Aaron should be punished for smacking Eben.

"We can't treat him differently," Mom said. "If Tess or Libby had done that, they'd have gotten in trouble for it. And what would the island think if I let this go? I'm Eben's teacher, as well as Aaron's foster parent. I can't be seen as favoring our own kids."

"What was Aaron *supposed* to do?" Dad asked. "Just take it? I bet it did Eben a world of good to be knocked down a peg."

Mom won in the end, though. I heard Dad's low rumbling voice in the attic a few minutes later, talking to Aaron.

I close my parents' bedroom door quietly, so we won't wake Mom with our kitchen noises. I tiptoe past Libby's door and step down the stairs, careful to miss all the creaky spots. Rushing into the kitchen, I say, "Let's go fishing!"

Dad swings around from the sink, coffeepot in his

hand. "Oh, glory, Tess! Are you trying to give me a heart attack?"

I grin. "I'm all set to go. Where's Aaron?"

"Have some breakfast." Dad pours coffee into his thermos, steam curling around his hand. "Mom made us some muffins last night."

Usually I love our early mornings together. The kitchen feels extra cozy and shadowy, with just the dim light on over the stove. It's like the house is barely awake, with only one eye open. But today I'm impatient to show off our lobster boat to Aaron. "Is Aaron awake yet?"

Dad screws the top on his thermos. "I think we should let him settle in today. He could probably use a quiet day, especially after yesterday."

"Eben asked for it."

"Even so, you can't go around hitting people. It's no way to solve things."

"But I bet Eben'll think twice before he messes with Aaron again."

"Let's hope so." Dad smiles, putting a couple apples in the cooler with our lunch. "Got warm socks on, Tess? It's chilly this morning."

"Warmest I've got."

"All right, then." He pulls his overshirt from its peg beside the kitchen door. "Let's go fishing."

As we cross the porch, Dad whistles softly, stroking his beard. He always says he has to get all the whistling out of him before he reaches the wharf, because it's bad luck to whistle on a boat. I hum along to the hymn "This Is My Father's World."

I slip my hand into Dad's big rough one. "Why isn't Aaron more excited to have a new home and a family?"

Dad stops whistling. "Give him time. This is all new and strange to him." He sighs. "Let me tell you something. When I picked Aaron up at the office the other day, he was waiting in a room with his trumpet and his suitcase. I said, 'Let's go home, Aaron,' but even as I said it, I knew it was the wrong word. He'd never been to our house before. How could he think of a place he'd never even seen as home?"

"What did Aaron do when you said that?"

"He asked me what name he should call me. I said he could call me Jacob or Dad or even Mr. Brooks, if he wanted. Then he picked up his things and followed me to the car—like it was no big deal." Dad shifts the cooler in his hand. "This is gonna take work, Tess. We've got to earn his trust. We need to be stubborn."

I tip my chin up to look at him. "I thought being stubborn was a bad thing."

He smiles. "Not always. Stubborn can also mean 'I won't give up on you.'"

"I'll be stubborn." Part of me itches to tell Dad about Aaron's letter. I want to know what it means that his mom wrote to him. But I also want to do what Dad said and earn Aaron's trust. If I tell, he'll never share anything else with me.

I peek to make sure Dad can't read my thoughts, but he's looking away now. I promised I wouldn't tell about Aaron's letter, but I didn't promise I wouldn't ask any questions. "Didn't Natalie say Aaron's mom and dad didn't care about him?"

"No! She didn't say that." He blows out an impatient breath. "She said he's never known his father, and his mother can't take care of him. That's not the same as not caring."

"Why can't she take care of him?"

"Because she's had lots of trouble with drugs and drinking. When people get hooked on things like that, they can't even take care of themselves, let alone their children." He glances at me. "That's just for you to know, Tess. Not to be repeated, not even to Libby. Okay?"

I nod. "Do you think Aaron's mom misses him?"

His fingers tighten over mine. "I expect so. It's very hard to know you've hurt someone you love. But his mom had a lot of chances to make this right, and she didn't do what she needed to. She didn't show up to meetings or take her drug tests. I guess the judge decided it was time to stop giving the chances to the parent and give them to the kid instead."

"But what if—"

"Look, Tess. We don't get a say in this. The State of Maine decided she can't have him, and unless they choose otherwise, that has to be good enough." He closes his mouth, done talking.

I hate when Dad does that, just clams up, like he's told me all I need to know. "The State of Maine says our school should be shut down. *That*'s not good enough."

"That's different," he says. "In our case, the State's *wrong*. They're only thinking about how much it all costs, but some things can't be undone. A long time ago, many of the islands in the bay had year-round communities. Now there are only six."

As we crest the hill, the bay stretches into view, strewn with islands. A few of the islands are long, with the roofs of houses poking up through the trees. But most are small and uninhabited, scraps of granite and pine.

I miss the days last summer when I could look at this view and feel happy, not scared I might lose it.

Against the pink sky, the smallest islands look like black, jagged-topped rocks tossed helter-skelter into the bay. I search out my favorites: Gosling Island and Big Goose next door, Hog Island, Baker, Pumpkin Knob, Pound of Tea, and the Three Sisters. A chain of three islands, the Sisters are connected at low tide but separated by water at high. When my skiff is launched, I hope I can talk Aaron into coming with me to the beach on the littlest Sister and walking all the way to the thick trees of the biggest one. I've always wanted to do that.

When you live on an island, a boat is freedom. You can go where you want and when you want, without worrying about the ferry schedule.

"Ready?" Dad asks. "Now!"

I pull in a sharp breath, filling myself down to my toes with clammy, early-morning mist and the damp taste of salt. We do this every day we go fishing — breathe in the morning together.

I hold my breath until my lungs feel ready to explode and my heart pounds a wild drumbeat in my ears. When I can't keep my air back one second longer, I nod at Dad and we let our breaths go together in a whoosh. "The Sisters aren't visiting," I say.

"Nope, but they'll be having lunch together. Low tide'll be about noon."

As we near the bait shack, I stop in my usual spot near the mailboxes. Bait stinks. It's a smell you get used to — briny and sickly sweet at the same time — but I'd still rather stand upwind while Dad drinks another cup of coffee and talks with the other fishermen on the wharf. He calls it his "catching-up cup." Today, I suspect the talk is of the new kids — especially Aaron.

Out in the bay, the *Tess Libby*, our lobster boat, waits on her mooring. It's always a comfort to see her there, her nose up and her wide, flat, open deck in the back. No matter how rough the seas are or how hard it rains, she stays right there, waiting for us.

Seems wrong to have a boat named half for Libby when she hates fishing. Hates the smell, hates the rocking of the boat, and especially hates the lobsters' wriggling legs. She's even afraid of the ocean itself, unless the sea's near glassy calm. "Libby didn't get the fishing gene," Dad says.

Not like me.

But whenever I ask Dad if he'll teach me to drive the *Tess Libby*, he always says no. And when I tell him I want to be a fisherman on my own someday, he says, "You're going to college. Spending the summer lobstering with me is okay while you're in school. But it's a hard, dangerous way to make a living, Tess. Harder'n I want for you."

"What about what *I* want for me?"

But Dad doesn't seem to think that question needs an answer. Waiting for him to finish catching up, I scan the bay, checking out the colorful lobster buoys to see where the other fishermen are setting. Some buoys are crowded together, marking the "hot spots" where lobsters are — or were. Others are sprinkled alone, just in case. I take special notice of Uncle Ned's yellow-and-red buoys and skip right over Eben Calder's orange-and-black ones. Eben's one of the "copycats." They follow the best fishermen around the bay and set their own traps nearby.

Dad and Uncle Ned have those copycats fooled, though. They each have a few buoys they use as decoys. Instead of a trap, the other end of the long rope is tied to a cement block at the bottom of the sea. Dad calls them his "new traps" and moves those cement blocks around the bay to throw off the copycats.

"Hey, *Tess Libby*, how's them new traps fishing?" Uncle Ned will ask Dad over the VHF.

"Haven't caught many lobsters," Dad will say back into the mic. "But I caught a bunch of fools."

I'd rather catch nothing than be accused of being a copycat. I look around for a new place to try setting my own traps. Near Sheep Island might be good. Not many fishermen are there — which may mean it's a dud. But the sea bottom around Sheep Island is plenty rocky, and if I were a lobster, I would pick somewhere with lots of underwater hiding places.

I reach into my pocket and pull out my newest good-luck charm: the piece of blue sea glass.

Let me choose the right place.

Then from behind me, I hear a sound I dread: the jingle-jangling of dog tags and the thudding of four big paws pounding up the road. Eben Calder's dog is one of those huge, angry-looking black dogs that make you want to cross to the other side of the road when you see him coming. A dog that thinks he's more *owner* than pet.

And if Beast's coming, so is —

"Hey, Mess."

I don't turn around — don't have to.

"Where's your bodyguard?" Eben asks.

I shoot a glare over my shoulder, but then my lips lift right up to a smile. Eben's jaw's all puffy on one side, making him look lopsided. "I don't need a bodyguard,"

I say, sweet as maple sugar. "Just a skinny trumpet player from the mainland is enough."

Eben narrows his eyes. "I'll get him back. You wait and see."

"Don't you dare!" I look for Dad, but he's over at the bait shack talking to Uncle Ned. "You're gonna ruin it for all of us, if you do."

"My dad says it's a stupid plan to take in other people's kids."

"That's because no one even *asked* your family to do it." I'm so mad I spit the last words. It's just a guess, but Eben's eyebrows fall, angry.

"My mom'll homeschool me if we lose the school, so I don't care," he says.

"Well, I do!"

"And my dad is already teaching me to drive our boat."

I clench my teeth so my jealousy won't show on my face.

"Tess!" Dad calls.

I'm relieved to get away from Eben, but as I hurry down the road, I get that prickly feeling between my shoulder blades, telling me he's watching me go.

I'm out of breath when I reach the wharf. "Can I drive the *Tess Libby* today? Just for a little bit?" I ask

Dad. "We could go way out where there's nothing to hit. Eben says his father —"

"No," Dad says, untying our skiff. "And I don't want you talking to Eben. He's caused our family enough problems this week."

"I didn't mean to talk to him. Words just kept popping out of my mouth."

"Next time, you keep those words in your mouth," Dad says. "Hear me?"

I nod. When I climb into the boat, boards sigh under my feet. I take my usual place in the stern.

As the skiff glides along, tiny whirlpools from Dad's oars rush past. "Time for our morning commute," he says.

I love how every day at the ocean is different — the clouds, the color of the water, the weather — it's never exactly the same. But today, I'm only thinking about what Eben said about getting back at Aaron.

Off starboard, a flight of cormorants huddles together on a ledge. Pitifully holding out their wings to dry, they look like a funeral group, all dressed in black with their arms out. Like they're begging heaven, "Take me instead."

"Do you think God ever makes mistakes?" I ask.

"Mistakes?"

"Like not giving cormorants enough oil to make their wings waterproof, so they have to stand there and dry them?"

Dad slows his rowing. "I wouldn't venture to speak for God, but maybe cormorants are the lucky ones."

"How so?"

"They have to stand still in the sun awhile every day," he says. "Not such a burden when you look at it that way. Might do some *people* well to stop running around and stand still awhile, too. Think so?"

I nod.

A seagull lands on the rock, shaking his wings. The cormorants pay him no mind, until he snaps at one. "I think that gull's making fun of the cormorants because they have to stand there with their wings out."

"Well, I wouldn't set much stock by seagull opinions," Dad says. "Any bird that'll eat rotten fish heads and garbage isn't someone to look up to."

I smile. "Shh. He'll hear you."

Dad shrugs. "I'm sure he's heard worse." As he pulls our skiff alongside the *Tess Libby*, I look over toward Eben getting into his father's lobster boat. I touch the blue sea glass in my pocket.

Don't let him make more trouble for us.

SEVEN

**A rainbow means
change is coming.**

We've been fishing several hours, when I decide to ask the question I've been wondering ever since Eben made his threat on the wharf. "Did Reverend Beal ask Eben's family to take in a foster child, too?"

"No. I'm sure he didn't," Dad says. "The Calders don't give enough attention to the kids they've already got."

As Dad puts the boat in gear, I sweep my gaze along Bethsaida: past the rooftops and the white church steeple poking over the trees, all the way to the gray gable and black roof of our house. Our attic window looks out over the treetops like a tiny, diamond-shaped eye. "Eben said he was gonna get Aaron back for hitting him."

"Hmmpf." Dad looks around me at his boat instruments. "Eben's all growl and no teeth." Everything about Dad's tight, though: his jaw, his knuckles, and the clench of his shoulders.

I put my hand on his sleeve. "But what if Eben does something else bad? Aaron might tell Natalie about it. Maybe she'll think we're all mean out here, even though it's only the Calders, and —"

"Tess! Will you *please* stop searching for trouble?" The annoyance in his voice slaps me. I lift my fingers, one by one, off his shirt. We bicker plenty, but he doesn't usually yell at me — not like that. If I were home, I'd run to my room and slam my door as hard as I could. But on a boat there's nowhere to go.

A seagull flies fast beside us, keeping up, as we pass the first of the Three Sisters. Pine and spruce trees crowd the islands, bunched together like spectators at a wrestling match. The first row of trees leans out over the water, the ones behind peeking over the front row's heads. A thin ribbon of water still flows between them.

Dad guns the engine, spray rising high along the hull.

"*Tess Libby*, you on?" Uncle Ned's voice comes over the VHF. "This is the *Windlass*. Barb wants to invite you all to supper soon — so you let us know when's a good time. Okay? And hey, Tess! How's it going?"

I glance across to the *Windlass* fishing at the far end of Bethsaida. A cloud of seagulls floats above the stern of Uncle Ned's boat, each gull swooping in and out of the others, trying to steal a mouthful of bait.

I don't really want to talk to anyone, but it'll be worse to explain. "Hey, Uncle Ned," I say into the mic, hoping if he hears the crack in my voice, he'll think it's radio static. "I'll tell Mom about Aunt Barb inviting us."

"Tess, who do you suppose your dad's trying to impress, driving like an idiot?" Uncle Ned laughs. "It couldn't be *us*, 'cause he already knows for a fact we ain't impressed with him."

Dad takes the mic from me. "Hey, boys. Looks like Ned's found a hot spot over near Cousins Island."

"You never mind where I'm fishing!" Uncle Ned says.

"Except he's setting so close to shore, he's as likely to catch chipmunks as lobsters," Dad says.

The easy teasing in his voice cuts me. If my family is forced to move to the mainland, Dad can still lobster out here on this same bay every day. His whole world won't change like mine will. I sit on a crate as far from him as I can get and pull my knees up under my chin.

"Cousins Island, huh?"

Whenever Dad and Uncle Ned start in teasing each other, fishermen all over the bay grab up their microphones and dive headlong into the scuffle.

"I've got a few traps I could put there."

"Red and yellow? Ain't them's your buoy colors, Ned?"

"Now look what you've done!" Uncle Ned snaps. "This is all your fault, Jacob."

"My fault?" Dad says. "How do you figure that?"

"Well, it ain't like I've figured the details yet!" Uncle Ned says. "But when I get to the bottom of it, I'll make sure it's your fault!"

Reaching over the boat rail, I dip my hand into the icy, needling spray. Within seconds my fingertips throb with cold. Droplets jump ahead of one another, racing near the hull. A scrap of rainbow flickers as sunlight passes through the wet mist.

A rainbow is a sign of change coming — which can be good luck or bad luck, depending on what kind of change you get.

Please let it be a good change.

Let it be Aaron changing to like it here. Or the school regulations changing. Or Dad changing.

Or — ? Peeking sideways through my fringe of bangs, I watch Eben hauling lobster traps with his dad near Gosling Island. Beast stands in the stern of their boat, nipping at the seagulls.

No, this tiny patch of rainbow can't be about Eben

changing. He'd need a *huge* rainbow — big enough for a complete overhaul. Dad might accuse me of searching for trouble, but there's one thing I know about trouble. It doesn't always sit around waiting to be found. Sometimes it comes looking for you.

"Tess, you tell your father my lobsters can whoop his lobsters any day of the week, even with one claw banded," Uncle Ned says. "You hear that, Jacob?"

"I heard it, but I don't believe it," Dad says. "Tess, you tell your uncle he's downright misinformed if he thinks I'd pit my burly lobsters against the scraggly little crawfish he's hauling today. Wouldn't be a fair fight."

The wind tickles my hair over my nose, and I tuck the strands back under my bandanna. My hair feels thicker with salt, and my skin is sticky.

The radio sputters. "*Tess Libby*, this is Kate," Mom says.

"I'm here, Kate," Dad says. "What is it?"

"Aaron would like to come join you."

Dad smiles, slowing the boat. "Sure."

I hold my breath so I can listen better. Aaron *wants* to come?

"We had a hard morning." Mom sounds tired, although it's not even lunchtime yet. "Natalie called to see how he was settling in, and Aaron asked for a visit with his mom."

I pull my fingers out of the water quickly. Did Aaron tell Natalie about his letter?

"Natalie said it isn't possible. And Libby has hardly let Aaron breathe today without her."

The defeat I hear in Mom's voice makes me worry maybe she's having second thoughts about all this. I grit my teeth. If Libby were here, I'd be tempted to push her overboard. I'm giving Aaron some space; why can't she?

"Don't worry. We'll swing by the wharf and pick him up," Dad says.

"He left a few minutes ago," Mom says. "In fact, he's probably almost there now."

Our wake churns a bubbly circle as Dad turns the wheel hard. Ahead on Bethsaida, a tiny truck drives along the shore road. Farther up, Jenna's mom stands in their doorway, letting their dog out. Laundry's being pegged on a clothesline at the Moodys' house as postage stamp–sized white sheets blow in the breeze.

And on the wharf, a red-haired boy waits.

EIGHT

The bad luck of having a redhead aboard can be averted if
you speak to the redhead before he speaks to you.

"Hook the gauge in the eye socket like this." Dad holds
the brass measuring gauge in his right hand and the
lobster in his left. "Lay it along the carapace — that's
the name for the lobster's back. See this point on the
gauge, Aaron? It has to fall on his back or he's too
small to keep."

I brace my legs against the rocking of the *Tess Libby*
and open the trap sitting on the boat's rail in front of
me. I haven't seen Aaron smile once since he stepped
on board.

"This lobster's a keeper, so the first thing we do is
band his claws," Dad continues. "That way he can't
hurt the other lobsters in the tank. They'll eat each
other, given half a chance."

Aaron steps backward away from the trap. "I'll
just watch."

"You're doing fine." Dad picks up the bander and puts a fat, ring-sized rubber band on the end. "The bander works like pliers—only in reverse. As you squeeze the handles, it spreads the rubber band open. See? When it's wide enough, you slip it over his claw." Dad holds the lobster and gives Aaron the bander.

My own catch isn't bad today, but I was hoping for better. Even though I called "Hi!" to Aaron before he came on board—hoping to undo his unlucky red hair by speaking to him before he spoke to me—Dad has outfished me good today.

I untangle a lobster from the netting of the trap in front of me. A lobster trap looks like a long, rectangular wire box with a brick or two in the bottom to even out the weight and keep it from flipping upside down in the water. There are two "rooms" inside, separated by a netted "head," with an opening in the middle for the lobster to crawl through and get stuck.

My lobster opens his claws at me, ready for battle.

"Much better," Dad says to Aaron. "Now *you* hold the lobster for the second claw. It's okay. Lobsters can't reach behind and grab you, the way crabs can. Just keep your hand back here." When Dad lets go, Aaron jerks his arm out, holding his lobster away from his body. Dad grins. "Gotta bring him a little closer."

As I squeeze my own bander, my lobster grabs the rubber band in his claw. "Hey, cut that out," I tell him.

The lobster thrashes, flipping his tail. I pick at the band, but he's got it clamped so tight it's a wonder he doesn't slice it in half. I set him on the deck to tire himself out. The lobster wriggles his spindly legs, but he can't get going. In water, lobsters scuttle easily along the sea bottom. They're graceful, dainty even. But on land, their bodies are too heavy and they have to pull themselves along, dragging their bellies.

The lobster opens his claw, and I snatch him up. "Gotcha!" I secure his fat crusher claw. As my lobster struggles to get that first band off, I slip another over his smaller pincher claw, easy as pie. "Gotcha twice!"

"Watch your fingers, Tess," Dad says.

My smile sags. Aaron may need to learn all these things, but I've been doing them right for years.

"We won't bother to measure this little one," Dad says, pulling a tiny lobster from the trap. "He's not even close."

I drop my own catch through the hole in the top of the tank. The water shudders as all the lobsters inside try to get out of one another's way.

"Hold out your hand, Aaron. He won't hurt you."

Dad lays the tiny lobster on Aaron's palm. "When Tess and I throw the short lobsters in, we always say, 'Today's your lucky day, little one.'"

I expect Aaron to make a disgusted face or squirm, but he pauses, holding the tiny lobster on the palm of his rubber glove. Leaning out over the rail, Aaron sets the lobster into a wave as gently as if he were made of glass. "Today's your lucky day, little one."

The lobster pauses just below the water's surface, his tiny claws outstretched. Then, flipping his tail, he spurts off backward, disappearing into the shadows under the boat.

Dad reaches back into the empty trap for the mesh bag of leftover bait. "Next we throw out the old bait, put in some new, and reset the trap. The bait bag hangs here in the first part of the trap — called the kitchen. The lobster comes into the kitchen to eat, and then he'll crawl up this ramp and through this opening between the two rooms. The back part of the trap is called the parlor, and that's where he gets stuck."

"Why doesn't he just leave the kitchen the same way he came in?" Aaron asks.

"I imagine some do," Dad says. "But climbing forward into the parlor is easier for him."

I hear a boat's engine behind us. I lift my hand to wave, until I see it's Eben and his dad — and Eben's driving their boat.

Dad opens the small, mesh bait bag and shakes the leftover fish bits into the sea. From rocks and ledges all around us, seagulls leap into flight. They dive-bomb through the air to pluck the bait bits off the waves, surrounding the boat in a swirl of wings and mournful cries.

Aaron jumps backward.

"They won't hurt you." I slide my gaze from Aaron's borrowed hauling pants to his life jacket and skinny shoulders to the ends of his red hair. When I reach his face, Aaron's eyebrows are so light-colored they don't seem to exist at a distance. But I'm close enough to see them go up in surprise. He opens his mouth and closes it twice, like he's struggling to keep from —

"Over the rail!" I yell, grabbing his arm.

We make it just in time. Which is a relief, because cleaning off our boat every night is bad enough without adding *that* in.

"Don't worry," Dad says, patting his back. "Everyone gets seasick sometimes."

I nod, though I've only ever felt queasy in the fog. When you can't see the horizon, your body plays tricks on you.

"I see the *Tess Libby*'s new sternman needs some weathering," Brett Calder says over the radio.

"Yeah," Eben adds. "Maybe the *Tess Libby* should be renamed the *Barf Bucket*."

I glance to Aaron. He's sitting on a crate with his head on his arms.

Dad picks up the mic. "Maybe you should pay more attention to your own boat and less to mine!" The back of Dad's neck is getting red. He snaps off the VHF. I don't remember him ever doing that before. He sometimes turns it down when he's sick of the chatter, but he never turns it off all together.

I make myself busy filling bait bags. Cloudy fish eyes stare up at me from the bait tub. I let my hands take over, grabbing slippery fish from the pile, cramming them into the bags.

Aaron looks so miserable that I peel off my rubber gloves and hunt around in the junk box Dad keeps on the boat. I push aside a little calendar the size of a credit card, a couple pencils, and some screws and nails, until I find what I'm looking for.

"It's spearmint. It'll take the taste out of your mouth," I tell him, laying a wrapped hard candy on his knee.

Aaron lifts his head just enough to look at me.

"It's gonna be okay," I promise.

Though I'm not sure either of us believes me.

NINE

**It's bad luck
to change a boat's name.**

At the end of two weeks, Aaron's getting his sea legs on the boat. Though he's still grabbing the dash or the rail every time Dad guns the engine, at least he's not throwing up anymore. After that first lobstering trip, I didn't think Aaron would ever want to leave land again, but I think he likes to be with Dad. Maybe it's because Dad doesn't talk as much as Mom and Libby and me. Or maybe it's that Aaron's a boy, and he hasn't had a dad before. I'm not sure of the exact reason, but Mom's noticed it, too. She even asked me to switch my seat at the supper table next to Dad, so Aaron can sit there.

I know *I'm* not the reason Aaron's coming on the boat. He hardly says a word to me. In the fourteen days he's been with us, I've suggested all kinds of fun things to Aaron. He's not a reader. He only likes to swim in a *lake*. He's not excited to meet the other kids on the island and doesn't want to play Monopoly with Libby and me. He said, "No, thanks," when I asked him if he wanted to try jumping off the ferry float into the ocean, and when I ask him what *he* wants to do, he says, "Nothing."

Nothing with *me*, he means.

So it's a surprise one afternoon to look up from scraping old paint off my skiff and see him walking toward me. I thought he was supposed to be having a meeting in our kitchen with Natalie, but he asks, "Want some help?"

I pause a few seconds in case he says, "Just kidding." But he looks serious, and anybody'd be a fool to turn down help scraping paint.

"Okay. There's another scraper in the shed. You'll see it in a box of stuff on the shelf inside the door."

The replacement wood Dad and I put on the skiff stands out new and raw-looking beside the ragged white paint of the old boards. Underneath the white's a layer of red paint and one of gray.

Aaron comes back with another scraper.

Paint flakes fall to my sneakers and onto the grass. "It's just an old wooden skiff," I say. "It's heavy as heck on land, but it won't feel that way in the water."

He nods. "Where'd you get it?"

Watching him start scraping, his hair swinging with each stroke, I feel a grin sneaking up on me. "It used to be my cousin Tom's. He got a new one, so I bought this one with some of my lobstering money from last year. It's not much to look at right now, but it's gonna be beautiful when it's done. I'm gonna paint it white, or maybe light gray like the fog. Dad makes me save most of my lobstering money for college, but I'm also saving up for an outboard motor so I won't have to row everywhere."

I'm talking way too much. I bite my bottom lip to keep it from saying anything else.

"Cool."

I think he really means it. There's no stopping that grin now. But I keep the "Yay!" to myself. "One of Dad's rules about kids and boats is Never go on the deep water alone. So maybe we can go together after it's launched and I can afford a motor for it."

He doesn't answer, just keeps scraping.

"I'm lucky Tom never named her, because now I get to. Sometimes I think it'd be good to have a funny name for it: *Pier Pressure*, *Go Fish*, or *Shore Thing*. Other days, I think it'd be fun to give it a pretty name, like *Wanderer*. I just have to make sure the name doesn't have thirteen letters, because that's bad luck for a boat."

The sound of our scrapers falls into rhythm together. I bite back the urge to keep chattering. The moment feels as fragile as a bubble — one prod too many and it's likely to break.

"Ouch!" Drawing his hand back, Aaron scratches at a tiny paint needle in his finger. Putting his finger across his mouth, he bites the sliver out.

"You want to hold the scraper like this." But before I can show him, he turns his head.

"I know how to do it."

He's still holding it wrong, but I don't say so. I wish I could ask him about his life before he came here and what else his mother's letter says. I want to ask if he likes us yet. Or if not, is there any chance he ever will?

But in "Your First Days at Home with Your Foster Child," it says, "Keep your questions to easy ones at first, like his favorite sports, TV shows, toys, ice cream, etc."

I sigh. "What's your favorite flavor of ice cream?"

He scrapes in long strokes, without looking at me. "I'm not hungry."

"That's okay. I don't actually have any ice cream." I feel completely stupid now, but having started this . . . "I'm just asking what you like."

"Oh." He pauses, and then starts scraping again, a little slower than before. "Cookie dough."

"My favorite is chocolate chip. Cookie dough would be somewhere in my top ten, though." I start scraping again.

"Come in now, Aaron," I hear Mom call. "Natalie is ready to see you." I look over to see Mom and Natalie on the porch. Why do they have to interrupt us *now*? I was finally getting somewhere with Aaron.

"Aaron!" Natalie calls. "How are you doing? Are you working on a boat? Wow! That's awesome."

He puts down the paint scraper and walks away from me. Almost to the house, he glances back over his shoulder. "Chocolate chip would be around number five for me."

As the kitchen door closes, I take my lucky things from my usual right-side pocket and put them into my left one. That little wrongness will nag at me, so I won't forget to write "cookie dough ice cream" on Mom's shopping list when I go inside.

I scrape extra hard on the spot where he got the splinter so it won't ever happen again. As I work, I can't help wondering what he's telling Natalie. Is he complaining about Eben being mean to him or getting seasick or Libby knocking on his door every night to see if he wants to play Monopoly? Is he telling Natalie how he still isn't comfortable opening the refrigerator or cupboards when he's hungry — how he pretends he doesn't want anything to eat until it's practically forced on him and then eats it all? Or how embarrassed he'll be going to school with kindergartners this fall? Or how much he hates the seagulls swooping around him on the boat?

Natalie's been here a long time — long enough to hear a whole long list of bad things from him.

I feel kind of cheated that Anne of Green Gables liked her island home right from the get-go and Aaron needs to be won over to his. I thought he'd feel more like Anne did, like it was a fun adventure to move here — not a punishment, a too-far-away-from-everything place where he has to give up what he loves best.

After Natalie leaves, I hear trumpet music coming from our house. It's a slow, sad song, the notes held long as sighs. He makes that trumpet sound both beautiful and hurt.

I put the scrapers back in the shed. I wish Aaron could find his place here, so he'd feel like a real islander and he'd start liking it more.

As I'm closing the shed door, I see Doris Varney bring her knitting basket out to the porch rocker. I notice she does that whenever Aaron starts practicing. "It's so nice to have a musician in the neighborhood!" she calls to me. "I wish everyone could be enjoying this fine music with us. Don't you? It'd be the talk of the island!"

And I have an idea.

"Hi, Mrs. Varney." I brush the paint dust off my clothes as I'm walking. "Isn't it great how Aaron plays the trumpet?"

"Oh, yes! I feel very lucky to hear such fine music from my front porch," Mrs. Varney replies, pulling out her knitting needles. "It's like having my own personal concert."

I let Mrs. Varney knit several rows on the blue mitten in her lap while Aaron finishes the song.

"It's a shame the whole island hasn't had a chance to hear Aaron," I say. "I bet everyone would really enjoy it. Don't you think so, Mrs. Varney?"

"Oh, yes. The boy plays like an angel!"

"And the trumpet is especially good for patriotic songs," I say. "Exciting, marching music, like we might hear at Memorial Day or the *Fourth of July picnic*."

I feel a little guilty doing this. I know Aaron said he didn't like to play for people, but he did once play in a jazz band. So he does play for people *sometimes*. If

Aaron could play his trumpet for everyone, they'd be amazed and tell him how wonderful it sounds and how great it is that he's here. Then Aaron'd see that he didn't have to give up being a musician — even if we don't have a jazz band.

"There's nothing like a trumpet for patriotic songs," Mrs. Varney agrees. "And for 'Taps,' too! That's always so moving. That song was played at my father's funeral. Did you know that? He was in World War II. It's been a while since I've heard that song played, but it always brings tears to my eyes. It reminds us of all those people who've sacrificed their lives for our freedoms, and — Where is my cell phone? I'm sure I put it in here."

As she hunts through her basket, I back away, smiling.

My work is done.

TEN

Never say "drowned"

at sea.

The next day, Dad, Aaron, and I've been fishing on the *Tess Libby* for about three hours when Mrs. Coombs's voice blasts over the boat's VHF: *"TESS LIBBY!* ARE YOU ON, JACOB?"

Mrs. Coombs never seems to understand that the radio's microphone means people'll hear her fine. She thinks she has to yell loud enough for people on the far side of the bay to listen in without even turning on their radios.

"JACOB BROOKS! I HAVE A QUESTION FOR YOU!"

The radio fizzles with static and then Uncle Ned's voice says, "Jacob, for pity's sake, answer her before we all go deaf."

"NED BROOKS! YOU KEEP YOUR NOSE OUT OF THIS! I'M TALKING TO YOUR BROTHER!"

"Shirley, this is Jacob." Dad turns the volume knob down. "What can I do for you?"

"Doris Varney said that boy of yours plays the trumpet. Is that true?"

"Ayuh," Dad says.

"I'm in charge of the entertainment for the Fourth of July picnic," Mrs. Coombs says. "The Ladies' Aid Society wants him to play us some stirring patriotic tunes while Reverend Beal cooks up the chicken barbeque."

Aaron stares at the VHF, as shocked as if it had burst into flames.

"You may as well say yes," I tell him, smiling. "Because Mrs. Coombs isn't really *asking*. She's just telling you to be there."

"'You're a Grand Old Flag' and 'Rally 'Round the Flag, Boys!'" Mrs. Coombs continued. "That's what we need, Jacob. None of this modern-day screaming nonsense like we had last year with Donnie Burgess and that electric guitar! It's a wonder Mrs. Ellis is still with us. It was enough to give someone her age heart failure —"

I slide my hand behind my back and cross my fingers for good luck. *Say yes, Aaron.* "It would mean a lot to everyone. Wouldn't it, Dad?"

He turns to Aaron. "What do you think?"

Aaron's eyes flash around him, like he's looking for a place to run. But unless he jumps overboard, he can't go anywhere. "I don't have any sheet music for those songs," he says finally.

"Can you find him some music to follow?" Dad asks into the mic.

"Of course!" Mrs. Coombs says. "I have a songbook here at home that'll do just fine. Send him over tonight after supper, Jacob. I'll have it all marked with what I want him to play."

I bite the inside of my cheek to keep from grinning as Dad hangs up the mic.

"Let's check how your traps are doing over near Sheep Island, Tess. Watch your feet, kids." As the boat pulls away, Dad pushes a trap off the rail, and I watch the rope attached to it unwind off the deck until it reaches the buoy tied at the end. The rope yanks the buoy into the water, marking the trap.

Across the waves lies the low, hazy hump of Sheep Island. The spot I've been fishing has proved okay, but I think there's a better one. "Today I'll move one of my traps a little ways farther into the channel between Sheep Island and Dead Man's Island," I tell Dad as he guns the engine.

Though both islands have been deserted for generations, Dead Man's is pitted with cellar holes — and a few even have stone chimneys still standing.

"Why's it called Dead Man's Island?" Aaron asks.

The concerned look in his eyes makes me want to tease him a little. "That's where we Bethsaida Islanders buried the people who didn't survive *last* year's Fourth of July picnic. Donnie Burgess and his electric guitar were never seen again."

Aaron's gaze turns on me, angry.

"I'm just joking," I add quickly.

"The story is that long ago a shipwrecked sailor washed up there," Dad says over the engine's roar. "There's a plain headstone for him in the cemetery over behind those trees. They didn't know what name to carve, so they left it blank."

I've heard that story plenty — Amy and I even told it to Libby a few times. Though when we told it, the islanders did lots more screaming and fainting at the horror of finding the dead body than when Dad tells it.

"Why didn't the man's family ever claim him?" Aaron asks. "Or at least tell people his name?"

"I don't imagine they ever knew what happened to him," Dad says.

Looking toward the island, I wonder if that sailor

did have people at home waiting. Hoping day after day, month after month, that he'd show up on their doorstep, older and tired, with an amazing story to tell.

People say it's better to know the truth, but what if the ending's a bad one? Is it still better to know? Or is it kinder to keep that string of hope dangling? To believe that maybe if you just wait long enough, everything could still end the way you want.

"What was the island called before the sailor came?" Aaron asks.

"Good question." Dad checks his boat instruments. "It probably had another name before then, but I guess everyone started calling it Dead Man's, and that's what stuck."

On the nearby rocky edge of tiny Sheep Island, a group of seals sun themselves. Their huge round bodies are stretched out, warm and drowsy. They raise their heads, curious, as we go by. A few more seals swim in the water between the island and our boat, the sun flashing off their wet fur.

"It doesn't make sense to name a whole island for a guy who didn't belong there," Aaron says. "I'm sure he didn't even *want* to be there."

"No, but it's where he stayed." Dad slows the boat

near my first buoy. He leans out to snag the buoy with the gaff, a long pole with a hook on the end.

As Dad starts the hauler, I head for the rail, but Aaron doesn't move. "My grandmother drowned, too," he says.

Below me, waves slosh against the hull and I half-expect them to rise up in white-capped fury and pull us down to the depths. Anyone who knows anything about the ocean knows you never, ever say the *D* word on a boat.

Though my first trap hasn't even broken the surface, Dad stops the hauler from pulling the trap up through the water. "Natalie said she had cancer?"

Aaron nods. "Fluid filled her lungs at the end. I didn't know a person could drown in a room full of air."

"I didn't know that either," Dad says quietly.

Every time I've allowed myself to imagine that unnamed sailor's last seconds, there was always a dark, cold ocean folding around him, and maybe a horrible patch of watery light way up overhead — never once had I thought of someone drowning from the *inside*.

Stripping off his rubber gloves, Dad drops each one on the deck. He puts his arm around Aaron and turns him into his shoulder. I expect Aaron to duck out from under Dad's arm or back away, but he leans his forehead, just enough to touch, against Dad's shoulder. Behind them, I feel alone and "extra," though I'm close enough to see every breath they take. I feel guilty for having an easier life than Aaron. For me, losing everything only means my home. I can't even imagine finding myself all alone, too.

"I'm sorry," Dad says. "You've been through more than any child should have to."

I step closer. I feel a little bad about Dad taking one hand off Aaron for me, but I need Dad right now, too.

In the water near our boat, a seal lifts his head up, locking eyes with mine. "Look, Aaron," I say.

He raises his head off Dad's shoulder just as the seal tucks into a dive, smooth as a wave.

"Wow," Aaron says.

"Don't let those big eyes fool you," Dad teases. "They're a bunch of thieves. Seals stick their heads into lobster traps and eat up the bait or the lobsters, sometimes ruining the trap in the process. So we fishermen have nothing good to say about them."

"*I'm* a fisherman," I say, "and I think they're beautiful."

"They have to eat, too," Aaron says quietly.

I nod. "That's right. They just want their supper."

"Will you still feel that way if one of those robbers has eaten your lobsters?" Dad asks me, picking up his gloves.

"Yes!" But when my trap is hauled, it's empty. Even the bait bag is gone. I shrug. "Anyone can have one bad-luck day."

"Or a good-luck day, if you're a seal," Aaron says.

It's so surprising to hear him joke that for a second I can't believe he really said it. "Yes, it's a *very* lucky day for a seal," I say.

And even Dad smiles.

ELEVEN

**You can reverse bad luck
by turning around three times counterclockwise.**

After supper, I take Aaron over to Mrs. Coombs's house to get the music book for the Fourth of July picnic. The cooling-down evening smells like Christmas trees and salt air. As we walk, I spin around counterclockwise to reverse the bad luck of Aaron saying "drowned" on the boat. When I twirl for the third time, he looks at me like I'm crazy. He should be grateful I'm protecting him, because bad luck is as real as good luck.

As we come up her walk, Mrs. Coombs opens her front door — before we've even knocked. I should've known she'd be watching for us.

"Hello!" I give her a wide, cheesy grin.

She narrows her eyes. Mrs. Coombs thinks any happy kid is up to no good. "I marked the songs for you to play." She hands Aaron a thick, spiral-bound music book, *Beloved Tunes of the American People*. A fringe of yellow Post-it notes juts from the pages. "I picked all the favorites."

I want to ask, *whose* favorites? But if I said that, Mom'd hear about it — probably even before I got home. Mrs. Coombs has the fastest phone-dialing finger in Maine. And I bet she has Mom on speed dial.

"Be at the picnic no later than eleven," she tells Aaron. "I'll borrow one of the music stands from church. We can set it up that morning on the parish hall steps."

"Okay," he says.

As Mrs. Coombs closes her door, Aaron sticks the songbook under his arm.

"It's nice of you to do this," I say. "Everyone will love it."

"I hate playing what other people want." He fingers the yellow bits of paper. "I probably don't even know half these songs."

"There's a piano in there." I point to the parish hall next door. "You could try the songs out. And if you don't know one, maybe I could hum it for you."

Aaron looks uncertain as he shifts the music book under his arm. "Don't they keep the door locked?"

"Not usually. There's nothing worth stealing in there, unless a thief wanted a load of bean supper plates and rummage sale stuff."

Aaron hurries across the lawn. He almost drops the music book as he runs.

"Wait! Don't walk on Mrs. Coombs's grass! She'll—" I glance back to the house, half-expecting to see her charge out of her front door, brandishing her phone.

Not even a curtain quivers in the window, so I run across the grass after him.

Inside the parish hall, Aaron sits at the black upright piano and dusts the keys with the bottom edge of his T-shirt. Then, striking a note, he wrinkles his nose. "Ouch."

"It doesn't get played much. Just for special events like the talent show or our island holiday party in December." My voice rings in the empty room, sounding like I'm more than one person. I flip light switches on and off until I find the one that controls the lights above the stage.

Today, that holiday party feels a world away. In the summer, it's easy to forget how frozen the air can feel out here in winter, like the sky itself could crack from it. Sea foam freezes into long lines and swirls on the shore, and any boats still left in the water wear skirts of ice each morning.

Aaron'll feel all settled in with us by *then*, I hope. He plays a chord, and a shiver runs between my shoulders. His face is serious, his eyebrows down and his eyes looking just above the keys. He plays three notes, and then repeats them. I imagine words to the notes, *"Come a-long. Come a-long."* Swaying gently side to side to the music, I watch the muscles in his forearms move as the song fills out, his right hand stretching up higher on the keys and his left hand crawling down lower. I wish I knew the real words — not that I would sing along, except in my head. "Where did you learn to play?"

"My grandmother had a piano. She taught me. I never knew I was a musician until I went to live with her. Then Home Number One had a keyboard."

The way he calls the place by a number tugs at me. I don't ever want to hear him call us Home Number Three.

"I was glad to leave that foster home. I missed my grandma, and I couldn't even get away from the other kids because I didn't have my own room. The only way I could be alone was to plug the headphones into the keyboard and play. I was only there a year, but it was long enough." He sets the music book on the piano's music stand. "I think they wanted a younger kid anyway."

"Where'd you get your trumpet from?" I ask, then

add quickly, "I mean who gave it to you?" hoping it didn't sound like I thought he stole it.

"When I was eight my caseworker at the time told me to write down what I wanted for Christmas. I wrote only 'a real trumpet' on my paper. I wanted an instrument I could play in the school band." He lifts one shoulder. "I was surprised when I really got one. Most Christmases, I wrote what I wanted, but then when the present came, it totally wasn't what I asked for — like one year I asked for a skateboard and I got a football instead. I don't even like football." Aaron starts a slow, bluesy piano melody. The low notes pound like waves rolling up and back on the rocks.

"That's really pretty music," I say. "No one in my family plays any instruments."

"Grandma told me my mom played piano a long time ago. I've never heard her, though."

"Has your mom ever heard you play?" I ask.

"No." He flips open the book to one of the Post-it notes. "I don't know 'You're a Grand Old Flag.'"

My mom would never miss seeing me in a concert. She'd write it on the calendar and be there in time to get a good seat. I imagine what it must be like for Aaron: standing up at the end as the audience applauds, but she's not there. Or unwrapping his trumpet that Christmas morning and not being able to hold it up and show her. Or seeing his birthday cake in front of him, and she's not telling him to make a wish. But it's all a big white blank in my imagination, because I can't even *pretend* what it would feel like not to have my mom at those times. "Couldn't she have just showed up at one of your school concerts?" I ask. "Even if it wasn't *technically* allowed. I mean, it's not like they check IDs at the door, right?"

"She never knew when the concerts were. And I couldn't tell her, because I didn't know where she was." He frowns. "Are you going to hum or not?"

I sigh and hum the first verse. I think I sound like a human kazoo, but Aaron nods his head in time with me.

"Have you written back to her?" I ask.

He shakes his head. "Every time I try, it comes out wrong — like I'm mad or I don't know what to say. I wish I could just talk to her."

"We could make your mom a video of the Fourth of July picnic," I say. "Then she could hear you play and see where you live now and meet Libby and me. We could show her cool things about the island."

"Your parents would have to ask Natalie. I hate how everything has to go through her. It's not like I'm a baby!"

"Well, what if —"

"Look, forget it! Okay?" he snaps. "I don't even know if my mom has a TV that works. Or a computer. Or whatever she'd need to watch a video."

I close my mouth. I feel bad that I kept asking questions and now he's upset. I wish I knew a good joke or something funny, to make him smile and take the anger out of his forehead. As Aaron plays the second verse of the song by himself, I glance to the stacks of boxes along the wall marked LADIES' AID SOCIETY RUMMAGE SALE. I don't think Aaron even sees me leave.

The clothes in the first box have a stale, old-people smell. I find a tweed sport coat and a wide blue-and-orange-striped tie. Sorting through sweaters, shirts, baseball caps, and a pair of ladies gloves so narrow I don't think they'd even fit Libby, I snatch up a slate-colored felt hat. The sort that snowmen wear.

"I'm sorry, sir. You do not meet our dress code." Holding the clothes out to Aaron, my chest seizes with panic. What if he sneers at me for acting babyish?

Taking one hand off the piano keys, Aaron holds his palm upward. "You couldn't pick a better tie?"

I smile, draping it over his hand.

Knotting the tie in place, Aaron gets up from the bench. From another box along the wall, he pulls out a knitted brown scarf with two huge, lime-green pom-poms at the bottom.

I'm not much for style, but that scarf is dirt ugly. Aaron wraps it loosely around my neck, flipping both ends over my shoulders. The pom-poms hit me in the back.

"Oh, how very *brown*." I pose with one hand on my hip. "What do you think?"

"Not quite." Aaron pulls out a purple sequined hat. He drops it on my head and tips it down on one side. "Better."

By the time we're done, Aaron's decked out in the tweed coat with his hat squashed low over his eyebrows, dark sunglasses, striped tie, and a rolled-up napkin for a cigar.

I'm wearing someone's raspberry-satin prom dress, bunched in my hand to keep it from dragging on the floor, the sequined hat, the brown scarf, and a whole jewelry box's worth of cheap, chunky necklaces.

Aaron sits back on the piano bench. "I'll play piano, you take the vocal part."

I smile, until I realize what he actually said. "Wait a minute! Do you mean actual words? I can't sing!"

"Everyone can. Some people are terrible at it, but everyone can sing." He flickers out a few twinkly notes on the piano. "Pretend you're someone else, then. That's what I do when everyone expects me to be someone I'm not." He glances at me. "The one, the only, the incredible —"

Oh, glory. "Um. Lola?"

Aaron grins, like I hoped he would. His left hand plays low notes, while his right hand passes me Mrs. Coombs's *Beloved Tunes of the American People*. "Pick one from here, Lola."

I flip through the pages. "Home on the Range" would sound ridiculous on Bethsaida, unless I substituted Eben's dog, Beast, for "buffalo." "Auld Lang Syne" isn't a summer song. And I don't even know "Sentimental Journey." "I think a better title for this book would be *Beloved Tunes of Really, Really Old People*."

I find a hymn I know from church.

"I don't know this one," Aaron says as I set the book open on the piano. "I'll follow you." He begins playing, slow and gentle. "You didn't take your cue, Lola." He begins again.

"I've got peace like a river," I sing so quiet I'm almost whispering.

I've got peace like a river
I've got peace like a river in my soul.

I've got peace like a river
I've got peace like a river
I've got peace like a river in my soul.

"Very pretty," Aaron says. "Keep going."

I've got joy like a fountain
I've got joy like a fountain
I've got joy like a fountain in my soul.
I've got joy like a fountain
I've got joy like a fountain
I've got joy like a fountain in my soul.

I've got love like an ocean
I've got love like an ocean
I've got love like an ocean in my soul.
I've got love like an ocean
I've got love like an ocean
I've got love like an ocean in my soul.

"You have good pitch," Aaron says.

"Yes, indeed. We could use you in the choir, Lola." Reverend Beal leans against the doorway, arms crossed.

I grab the purple hat off my head. "We were just —"

"How about 'Amazing Grace' now?" Reverend Beal asks. "We really, really old people like that one."

I clamp my fingers over my mouth.

"I got a call from Mrs. Coombs. She saw you two come in here and was worried you were up to mischief." He glances at the open boxes.

"We'll put these things back neatly," I say. "I promise."

"All in good time." Reverend Beal sets up a folding chair and sits down to be our audience. "I think Fourth of July will be very special this year," he says. "Thank you for agreeing to play for us, Aaron."

As Aaron plays "Amazing Grace," Reverend Beal joins in with his booming bass voice. I let myself sing a little louder with each few words, in a way I never would dare at church or school, where I try to keep my voice low and in the middle of the group.

Aaron plays verse after verse.

And I sing free.

TWELVE

To learn when something will happen, pull off
a daisy's petals, one by one, while saying, "This year, next
year, sometime, never." The last petal tells the answer.

On the morning of the Fourth of July picnic, Dad and
Libby go to the parish hall to help decorate. Last year,
Amy and I were in charge of decorating all the long
tables, but when Dad mentioned going this morning, it
didn't sound fun without her.

I'm washing up breakfast dishes with Mom to the
far-off sound of Aaron improvising with his trumpet
in the attic.

You're a grand old flag, do-doot-de-doo!

From the open window above our kitchen sink, I
watch the spruce treetops swaying in the breeze, like
they're dancing. Thin clouds stretch a line of dashes
across the blue sky. And past our yard, Doris Varney
sits in her porch rocker, a mug stopped halfway to
her lips.

You're a high-flying flaaag!!

"You don't think Aaron'll play it that way at the picnic, do you?" Mom pulls a dry dish towel from the rack beside me. "Because Mrs. Coombs will be fit to be tied."

I rinse a skillet under the water. "I like the song that way."

You're the emblem of —
the land I looooove.

"It makes it sound new and not as ordinary." I hand the skillet to Mom and pick up a juice glass from the soapy water. "He also plays the piano really well. Did you know that?"

"No. Is that why you two were sneaking around the parish hall the other day?"

"Um." I scrub the glass so hard it squeaks.

Mom smiles. "Mrs. Coombs called, but I told her you wouldn't be up to any trouble. I'm so glad Aaron's feeling more a part of things here."

The home of the free and the brave! BAH-dah-DAH!

"I can't wait for everyone to hear Aaron play." Part of me is itching to tell Mom this was all my idea and how I got Doris Varney to call Mrs. Coombs — without me even asking her. I'm afraid Mom might think that was meddling in other people's business, though, instead of helping out. But sometimes the right thing needs a little shove to get started.

Keep your eye on the grand old flaaaaaaag!

The long church supper tables are set up on the grass, covered with pies, cobblers, and slabs of watermelon on paper plates. The Ladies' Aid Society went red, white, and blue wild this year — from the striped napkins on the table to the little flags stuck upright in the cupcakes to the balloon bouquet attached to the fire hydrant. There are buntings under every window and twisted streamers looped over the parish hall doorway.

Dad's over with the men tending the clambake, and Reverend Beal, wearing a chef's apron, bastes and turns chicken legs on the big grills. All around, women hurry with platters and bowls and shoo the littlest children out from underfoot.

Mom, Aaron, and I make our way around a traffic jam of old ladies:

"Let's make some room on the table for this."

"Do we need a bowl for the chips or can we just put out the bag?"

"Oh! Who brought this blueberry pie?"

Mrs. Coombs calls over to Mom, "Isn't this a beautiful day, Kate? We couldn't have had better weather if we'd ordered it from a catalog!"

"Yes," Mom replies. "It's a perfect day for a picnic — sunny, but with that lovely breeze off the water to keep the mosquitoes away."

"I'm glad you remembered my music book, because I've thought of a few more songs I want to add." Mrs. Coombs nods to Aaron. "You can come over and get ready. No funny business, now — I want those songs played with the respect they deserve."

"Don't worry," Aaron mutters, handing her the songbook. "I'll play everything downright grim."

He follows Mrs. Coombs, and I sidestep a few people setting up folding chairs.

Next to the lemonade table, I see Mrs. Ross with her hand on Grace's hair. I scan the crowd to see if all the other new kids are here, too. I see Henry setting up chairs with Mr. Morrell. The Webbers brought Sam, and — oh.

Over to one side, Eben Calder is sitting with a group of summer kids. Eben nods his head toward me and says something to the boy next to him. The boy laughs.

I make a sour face at them. Eben better not make any trouble today.

As I pass the dessert table, I pull a daisy from one of the vases of red carnations, white daisies, and blue iris.

When will I know for sure that Aaron will stay with us? I start pulling off petals. *This year, next year, sometime, never. This year, next year, sometime, never.* I pull petal after petal, ending with *sometime.*

I drop the bare stem in the grass. "Sometime" could include "this summer," right?

"Hey, Tess," Jenna says, coming up beside me. "You'd better act busy or Mrs. Coombs'll pick a job for you. Last year she put me in charge of picking up trash. It was disgusting."

I smile. "Okay."

We rake seaweed over the clams for Dad and carry things for Reverend Beal. As we work, I keep sneaking glances to Aaron talking to people and getting ready. This is gonna be great! As he opens his trumpet case, I tell Jenna, "Come on. It's starting!"

"Aaron's real good at trumpeting," Libby announces loudly as Jenna and I sit down between her and Grace on a blanket on the grass.

"He's *more* than good," I say.

Mrs. Coombs picks up her songbook off the table. She carries a music stand to the top of the parish hall steps and sets it dead center in front of the audience. "Welcome, everyone! We have a special treat today! Aaron has agreed to play us some good old-fashioned patriotic tunes to get our toes tapping!"

I glance to Eben whispering with another boy on the other side of the lawn, his full plate balanced on his knee. Eben probably just came for the free food.

Aaron stands up straight, his fingers flickering over his trumpet stops. I would've expected him to look embarrassed by Mrs. Coombs's corny introduction, but he just straightens the music book on the stand.

Libby inches forward on the blanket, and I throw a proud look at Eben. He gives me a mocking smile, but it doesn't bother me one bit. It feels like when I play UNO with Libby, and I'm down to one wild card left. I sit there, waiting to lay that last card on the table and win.

"So let's give Aaron a big Bethsaida Island welcome for agreeing to entertain us this day!" Mrs. Coombs says.

People clap politely. Aaron steps his feet apart, like he needs to brace himself against the music. His elbows come up, his forehead lines with concentration. He purses his lips at his mouthpiece.

My country, 'tis of thee,
sweet land of liberty, of thee I sing;

For the first few notes, I don't recognize the song. Aaron plays it soothing, like a lullaby.

Land where my fathers died,
land of the pilgrims' pride,
from every mountainside let freedom ring!

Mrs. Ellis starts singing along from the audience, her quivery old voice sounding surprisingly good with Aaron's trumpet.

My native country, thee,
land of the noble free, thy name I love;
I love thy rocks and rills,
thy woods and templed hills;
my heart with rapture thrills, like that above.

Let music swell the breeze,
and ring from all the trees sweet freedom's song;

let mortal tongues awake;
let all that breathe partake;
let rocks their silence break, the sound prolong.

Our fathers' God, to thee,
author of liberty, to thee we sing;
long may our land be bright
with freedom's holy light;
protect us by thy might, great God, our King.

Everyone claps loud and long. Libby inches forward on the blanket, and I glance at Eben. He stares back, but I don't care, because I know Aaron's good and so does everyone else.

Aaron smiles, looking happier than I've ever seen him, and turns the page of the songbook. He plays "Pilot's Hymn," "God Bless America," and "The Battle Cry of Freedom."

Sitting cross-legged on the ground, I roll a piece of grass between my finger and thumb. Mom didn't need to worry about Aaron improvising, because he plays song after song without a single "doo-wah." But I miss the spirit he gives those songs at home — the extra bits he adds that lift them up to something new.

With every song he plays, more people sing with him. My toes move gently up and down in my sneakers. When he holds a long note, he closes his eyes for a moment, his muscles tight in his arms and around his mouth. Leaning back, he tips his trumpet up, like he's playing that note to the trees. As he finishes each song, I cross my fingers it won't be the last.

In the pause after "Stars and Stripes Forever," I hear Mrs. Coombs from somewhere behind me. "Wasn't that stirring, Kate? I always said Aaron would be a good addition to this place."

I can't see Mom, but I bet she's pursing her lips, holding back words — like I am. Except Mom's words probably don't include "old biddy."

"Such a fine young man, even if he is a bit scruffy around the edges," Mrs. Coombs continues. "A good haircut, that's all he needs."

Aaron turns to another bookmarked page. His eyebrows shoot up and his mouth opens. His gaze sweeps over the audience. Then he slams the songbook shut so hard, the music stand teeters.

Everyone claps, but Aaron's off the steps and cutting through the maze of people on the grass. Wait! He didn't play "Taps" yet. He knows Mrs. Varney is waiting especially for that one.

"What's going on?" Libby asks Jenna as I scramble over purses and blanket corners and squeeze past elbows. Dad and Mom stand up, but Aaron doesn't even stop for them. "Excuse me," I say over and over.

Ahead of me, Aaron runs away down the road. His shoulders are hunched and his head dips forward, like he's hurrying headlong into a storm, with his trumpet under his arm. I call after him, but he doesn't look back — not once.

THIRTEEN

Never paint a boat blue.
The sea will think it belongs to her and take it as her own.

On an island, silence usually means people are talking about *you*. Our phone hasn't rung since we got home. The whole island's probably hashing over how Aaron stormed off and about the Post-it note Mrs. Coombs found on the bookmarked page of "Taps."

Go home!

Oops, you can't. Right, orphan?

"At least he didn't punch anyone," Libby said to Mom and Dad when Aaron wouldn't come down for supper.

"I'm going over there and have it out with Eben and his father," Dad said, pushing back his chair.

"You don't know if Eben did this," Mom replied. "You let me handle it. You and Brett Calder'll just make this worse."

They argued about it until Dad stormed off to Uncle Ned and Aunt Barb's house, and Mom went upstairs to talk to Aaron.

I think she did most of the talking, though.

When Mom came back downstairs, I went to my room and listened hard to hear how Aaron was taking this: Would he cry or throw things or even pace in the attic above my room? But I didn't hear anything at all, and that felt sadder than if he'd been sobbing.

In the morning, Mom got a call from Mrs. Coombs, saying she'd discovered that Eben was at the bottom of that note. She'd gone straight over to the Calders' house and given him a big piece of her mind and now he has to mow the whole cemetery as a punishment.

"I suspect that'll set Eben straight," Mom said after she hung up the phone.

I doubt it, though. I can't imagine Eben's a bit sorry.

Aaron doesn't leave his room until I'm out working on my skiff. From under my fringe of bangs I see him coming. He's frowning, not looking at all like he's in the mood for talking. He takes a paint scraper, and we work in silence. I'm about half done with the scraping. Most of the boat looks shabby and old right now, but sometimes you have to make things worse in order to make them better.

Aaron chips at the paint so hard, he takes some wood off with it.

"Hey!" I say.

He does it again, and another sliver of wood flies off the hull.

"Stop it!" I grab for the paint scraper.

He pulls the tool away before I can get it. "This part'll be in the water. No one'll even know."

"*I'll* know!"

He lowers his eyebrows, but I don't back down. "Look, I'm sorry Eben put that note in the music book. And I'm sorry if my family isn't doing everything right, but we really are trying, and we want you to fit in here. Why didn't you just crumple up the note and throw it away?"

"I showed up and I played — even though I didn't really want to! Isn't that *enough*?" He glares at me. "You went to that picnic because everyone knew you belonged there. I only got invited to play the trumpet!"

"That's not true! You would've come with us, even if you didn't play."

"Right. I would've come with *your* family! And if you didn't need me to keep your school open, I wouldn't even be here." He gouges another splinter of wood off my boat.

I snatch the scraper from him. "So what? That doesn't mean it has to be awful or that we don't want you. Everybody gets something for the things they do.

Even when people *seem* like they're only thinking of others, maybe it's because doing good makes them feel nice inside. Did you ever think of that? Those people are still getting something in return. Maybe we're just more honest about it."

Aaron huffs. "You have no idea what it's like for me. Not being where I want to be, having everything I've known yanked away from me, over and over. Having people feel sorry for me or think I'm a bad kid because something bad happened to me. You can't even imagine it."

"Maybe not as much as you," I say. "But since last winter, I've been imagining losing things that matter to me — having to start over at a new school, coming into the middle of everything where kids have made all their friends already. Having to learn all those people's names, and I will have missed how they learned to do everything. And because everyone else *knows*, no one will think to explain it to me."

"You mean like what happens to *me* every time I have to move? Except I have to do more than change houses and schools. I get dumped into a whole new family each time."

His words smack me. "I'm sorry."

"Forget it. When your skiff is ready, I'm—" He stops.

"You're what?" I wait, but he doesn't answer. "What do you mean when my skiff is ready?"

He still won't answer, but he makes a fist so tight I see blue veins bulging on the back of his hand.

How could I have been so stupid? "I thought you wanted to work on this boat so you could do something with me."

"I want my own home again—with my own mom. Why can't you understand that? I thought you wanted to be my friend."

I lay both scrapers down on the hull. "I do. But—"

"When they came and took me away that first time, the lady promised it'd all work out in a month or two." He flicks at a stubborn paint chip with his fingernail. "What a joke."

"But if your mom didn't do what she was supposed to—"

"They made it too hard for her!" He picks up one of the scrapers and stabs the boat with the corner hard enough that it stays upright, stuck in the wood. "They could've tried something else or given her another chance. Mom didn't give up—they did!"

"But you can't run away with my skiff! They'll just come find you and —"

"I should've known you'd take their side!"

"I'm not taking their side!" I say, even though he's already walking away from me. "But don't expect me to keep this secret, too."

I grab the handle of his scraper and pull the blade out. As I'm smoothing over the cut in the wood, the screen door slams.

FOURTEEN

**Touching wood brings
good luck.**

As I climb the steps to the porch, I hear Mom talking in the kitchen. "Aaron's going through a hard time. I'll play Monopoly with you instead."

"But he *never* plays with me!" Libby whines. "I keep asking and asking, and he keeps saying no, no, no."

I take a tiny step backward from the door. I want to tell Mom about Aaron's plan to run away, but I want to do it alone.

"I said he could come live with us, but I didn't know he'd hate me!" Libby says.

"I'm sure he doesn't hate you, honey." After a pause, Mom adds, "He's not used to having little sisters. And he's been moved around so much, it's probably hard to believe he's here to stay. Saying good-bye is always hard, Libby. Maybe it seems easier not to get too close to us, in case that happens again."

I slump against the side of the house and stare out at my skiff. How can I ever launch it now? All this time, I was hoping Aaron'd be a boy version of Anne of Green Gables, but Gilly Hopkins came instead: angry and tough and not wanting to need anyone.

I liked that book, *The Great Gilly Hopkins* — all except the ending. In the book, Gilly had come to love her foster mom, but one day Gilly got mad and wrote a complaining letter to her birth mom. That mom came and took her back. Why couldn't Gilly realize how good she had it before she threw it all away?

"I should have guessed that holidays are probably extra hard for him," Mom says to Libby. "Seeing all those families together."

"But aren't we his family now?"

"You don't forget people you love, even when you don't see them," Mom says. "Though in some ways it might be nice if he *could* have a visit with his mother. It's easy to remember only the good parts of people if you never see them. Real people are much more complicated."

Hmm. I turn to stare at the doorknob of the screen door.

"Maybe Tess will play Monopoly with you." I hear a kitchen chair scraping as it's pushed back.

Oh, glory! I jump over the porch rail to the ground. I don't want Mom to catch me eavesdropping, and I sure don't want to be stuck playing hours of Monopoly with Libby. Racing around the corner, I cut it so close that I graze my arm on the wood.

Touching wood is usually lucky, but this time it hurts, too. Though I don't mind too much, because I need every bit of good luck I can get right now — even if it comes with some scratches. Holding my elbow to my chest, I open our front door and slip inside.

Mom said it herself — maybe it would be a good thing if Aaron could see his mother. Then he could find out that she's not only made of the good parts he remembers. And his mom can see that he's fine with my family and how we can give him things she can't or maybe doesn't want to. When Gilly first saw her biological mom again, she wanted to change her mind. The same thing will happen for Aaron, I'm sure as certain. Like Mom said: Real people are complicated.

I head for Aaron's room. It's weird to think I used to go up to the attic whenever I wanted and now I have to knock. No one answers, so I open the door. But when I climb the stairs to the attic, Aaron's room is empty. His suitcase, his trumpet, his music stand, and the photos on his dresser are gone.

FIFTEEN

**If you find a button on the ground,
walk around it clockwise three times
to remove its bad luck before you pick it up.**

Out of breath from running hard, I'm relieved to see his red hair. Aaron's sitting on his suitcase on the little scrap of beach beside the ferry landing. His trumpet case rests on the sand at his feet and he's wearing his leather jacket, even though it's past seventy degrees out. He doesn't even glance at me as I walk over and lean against the big rocks beside him.

"Why are you down here on the beach?" I pant the words out.

Across the water, the ferry has left the mainland wharf and is about a third of the way to this island, its bow pointed toward Bethsaida.

Aaron frowns. "I don't want to talk to anyone on the wharf. I want to sit here all by myself until the ferry shows up and then go home."

"It won't work," I say gently. "The ferry captain won't take you over across without calling Dad first.

An island kid can't just get on the ferry by himself with a suitcase and not have to answer some questions."

"I'm not an island kid."

A winged shadow sweeps the sand. I look up to see an osprey soaring past, barely moving his wings, carried on air.

Aaron picks at the handle of his suitcase with his fingernail. "No one's going to decide things for me anymore. I'm getting off this island and going home — even if I have to swim!"

I give him a tiny smile. "Salt water will ruin your trumpet."

He glares at me — a look I've only ever seen him give to Eben.

The corners of my lips fall. "I'm sorry. You're right. There's nothing funny about this."

A lazy wave comes up the sand. Aaron moves his things backward, away from it, but I point my toes to touch it. The water comes fast, circling my ankle before shrinking down the beach, rolling a clump of seaweed with it. A tiny white crab scuttles sideways on the wet sand, making footprints so light I can barely see them. He scurries past a fray of red-and-white rope, some kelp, a little green lobster band, and —?

A button.

It's not much, but I want to give Aaron something. Before I reach down to pick up the button, I walk around it clockwise — once, twice, three times to take away any bad luck leftover from the previous owner. I go around one more time to put some good luck in.

The button was probably gold-colored once, but salt water has worn the shine off the surface and the tiny wreath of leaves circling the front. I shake it in my closed fist to bounce the sand away. "Here," I say, holding it out to Aaron.

He doesn't take it.

I lean close enough to drop it into his jacket pocket. "I made it lucky for you."

He reaches into his pocket, and I hold my breath, half-expecting him to hurl the button away. Looking down at his hand, he runs his thumb over the button's tiny leaves. "I just want what you have, you know. My own family. Even if it's not perfect — it's mine."

He drops the button on the sand, like it's trash. "They didn't have to take me away from my mom. I could've taken care of her."

Looking down, I feel discarded by him, too. "You were Libby's age."

"I could've tried! And I'm older now. I don't need as much as I did when I was little. I could help her out more." He nudges a clump of rockweed at his feet. Underneath is a cluster of purple-blue mussels, still tightly closed. Reaching down, he untangles one from the seaweed. "I don't know why I can't even see her. I mean, how could that hurt anything?"

"Did you ever finish your letter back to her?"

He shakes his head. "I've tried, but I have to know for sure that she's okay and ask her if she's going to try to get me back. I can't write that in a letter. I have to *see* her."

I glance toward the ferry, close enough now for me to see separate colors: the blue hull, white wheelhouse, and the red benches on the upper deck. I'll never talk Aaron out of this. As long as he has that string of hope dangling that he'll be happier with his mother and that she'll be everything he's missing, we won't ever be enough.

When I turn back, Aaron is heading for the water, his arm crooked, holding a pile of mussel shells against his ribs.

I move his suitcase and trumpet farther up the sand, out of reach of the incoming tide. "What are you doing?" I ask, hurrying to catch up to him.

"I'm saving these from the seagulls. They don't have to die." At the water's edge, he throws a mussel. It skims the surface before slicing into a wave. He pitches another, farther out.

I swallow hard. "I was thinking about the talent show —?"

He throws another mussel, harder. "I'm not playing for any island thing ever again!"

"Not even if your mom came?"

He pitches his next mussel, but not as far out. His shoulder closest to me lifts forward.

"That show is open to the public," I say.

When he turns, I pretend the sun is in my eyes. I feel terrible that I'm setting him up to be disappointed in her — but it'll be a good thing in the end. "She could just show up. Nobody here has met your mom — well, except *you*, of course. If she came, everyone'd think she was just a tourist coming to watch the show."

"I don't want Mom to get in trouble."

"Don't you think she'll get in *more* trouble if you show up on her doorstep?" I ask.

He looks down at the mussels still piled against his chest. His hair swings forward, hiding his face. "I don't even know if she *has* a doorstep. She didn't say in her letter if she has a house or an apartment or if she's living by herself or with other people. I'm afraid if anything bad happened to her, no one would even tell me."

"Natalie has never mentioned your mom to me," I say gently. "So it can't be breaking a rule for *me* to invite her, right? You could give me her address off the letter she sent, and I could write her and give her the details. Then if she shows up —"

"She *will* show up," Aaron says firmly.

"Then you can see her and she can see that you're okay and no one needs to know or get in trouble."

He looks out at the ferry, close enough that one of the passengers waves to us. "You'll give her all the details about the ferry?" Aaron asks. "I don't think she'd know how to get here."

"Sure. I'll send her a ferry schedule and a map."

"Can I play whatever I want at the show?"

I nod, holding my hand out for a mussel. "Anything at all."

He puts one on my palm. I run my finger over the shell, wiping the sand away. Aaron throws his last mussel far into the water. "Okay." He turns and walks back up the beach.

As he picks up his suitcase and trumpet case, I throw my mussel into the water after his, as hard as I can — so far I barely see the splash.

"Today's your lucky day, little one," I whisper.

SIXTEEN

If you write your wish beneath the
stamp on a letter, the letter will
carry the wish with it.

Alone at my desk, I pull forward a sheet of paper.

Dear Ms. Spinney,
You don't know me, but my name is Tess Brooks. I am
Aaron's

I put the top of my pen in my mouth and slide it
slowly across my teeth. I don't want to say "foster sister." It sounds second best.

I get another piece of paper.

Dear Ms. Spinney,
Hi! How are you? Your son, Aaron, lives with my family on
Bethsaida Island in Maine.

The "lives with my family" sounds like he's renting

a room here. But if I said he's *in* my family, would she get mad since he's her kid, too?

I don't think the right words have been invented for this situation yet. I didn't realize how hard this letter would be to write. I feel a bit grumpy with her, too. She hurt him.

But I can't scare her out of coming. I move my pen down to the next line.

Aaron is a ~~good~~ great trumpet player. He's also helping me with my boat and learning how to go lobstering without throwing up.

Why'd I bring *that* up? I drum my fingers on my desk. Then I get a clean sheet of paper.

Dear Ms. Spinney,

Hello. My name is Tess Brooks, and I am eleven years old. Your son, Aaron, came to live with my family several weeks ago. He would like to see you, but it's not allowed.

I've been thinking about this, and I have an idea. We live on Bethsaida Island in Maine, and we get lots of tourists here in the summer. So we're used to seeing strangers on the ferry and walking around the island.

We have an island talent show on August 15th at 2:00 pm at the parish hall, and if you came and sat in the back of the audience and maybe called yourself a tourist (which you <u>would</u> be, since you don't live here—so it's not technically lying), Aaron could see you and you could see him. And no one would get in trouble.

He wanted to run away to see you, and I think you'll agree that's not a good plan. So maybe this could work out?

Sincerely,
Tess Brooks

P.S. He's playing his trumpet in the show for you—he's really, really good.

P.P.S. I'm enclosing a ferry schedule and a map of the island with the parish hall marked.

P.P.P.S. Could you also wear a little disguise? Just in case? Nothing too extreme (like a false mustache) but maybe sunglasses and/or a wig?

I write the address on an envelope and fold up my letter small enough to fit. If you write your wish beneath the stamp on a letter, the letter will carry the wish with it. Without even pausing to think, I write under the stamp:

Please come.

SEVENTEEN

**For good luck, blow on dice
before you roll.**

Summer is short and changeable in Maine — like the
weather can't make up its mind. One day it can be
ninety degrees, so hot in the sun that rivers of sweat
trickle down my spine and my rubberized hauling
pants stick to my skin wherever they touch it. A week
later, it can turn so chilly and foggy that I'll need jeans
and a sweatshirt. The talk at the store is always the
weather and the Red Sox — starting with whichever
one is doing worse.

Because summers are so short, each day feels extra
urgent, like you'd better grab it and enjoy it before it
slides away into fall and winter again. *Slow down*, I want
to say, to keep time from going too fast. I don't want to
think about how it's almost August already.

Like the weather, I feel like I'm just waiting to
see what'll come next. Eben hasn't caused any new
problems, but I don't trust him. And I mailed Aaron's

mom's letter three weeks ago, and she still hasn't written back. "Don't worry," Aaron keeps telling me. "She'll come."

"Aha! Now I've got all the railroads," Libby says one stormy afternoon, grabbing the stack of Monopoly property cards to hunt for the last railroad. "And you haven't got any." She stretches "any" extra long.

I cross my arms. "Of course I don't have any railroads if you've got *all* of them. Otherwise it doesn't make sense."

Libby and I have been sitting on the living room floor long enough that my back is starting to hurt. I can stand for hours on the boat and not feel it, but sitting's a different story. Dad and I'll fish in the rain and even in the fog, but heavy wind or lightning keeps us ashore. So when Dad said, "Not today," about fishing, Mom said it "would be nice" if I'd play Monopoly with Libby instead. "And let her be the banker," Mom said. "It's good math practice for her."

When Mom says something "would be nice," it sounds like you have a choice, but really you don't.

I blow on the dice for luck and roll an eight. Libby is winning because she has all the yellows: Marvin Gardens, Ventnor Avenue, and Atlantic Avenue, and she's closing in on the reds. All she needs is Kentucky

Avenue and then she'll have that whole side of the board. When Libby was littler I used to let her win, but now she does it on her own.

I have Boardwalk, and if I can get Park Place, I might be able to turn this game around. Picking up my tiny ship, I move eight spaces to Chance.

Chance and Community Chest are tricky, because you're as likely to get bad news as good. I pick up the orange card. Libby twists her head, trying to see underneath. Putting my hand across the bottom, I lift up one corner to peek myself. The bald Monopoly man is smiling. Whew. "Bank pays me fifty dollars!"

Libby frowns, giving me a blue fifty from the bank. She rolls the dice and makes her little dog stomp down the board so hard the small green plastic buildings slide off their colored bars.

"Hey, cut it out. You're making all my houses shake."

"It's an earthquake!" Libby slides her token around the Just Visiting corner at the jail and lands firmly on States Avenue.

"Ding-dong! It's the landlord calling!" I tell her. "That's mine. You owe me ten dollars."

I hold out my hand for it, but Libby is looking over my shoulder toward the kitchen door. "Wanna play?"

"No," Aaron says. "That's okay. You've already been playing awhile."

But his voice has a little twist of "maybe" in it. I pick up the stack of properties. "That doesn't matter. We'll start you with some property and some money so you can catch up."

"Don't give him the last red one," Libby says. "I'm saving up for when I land on that one."

"That's the *first* one I'm giving him." I lay some piles of money and the rest of the property cards, including Kentucky Avenue and Park Place, across the board from me. "Aaron, you have to play. Otherwise, I'm sunk."

He sways a little in the doorway. His chest seems to be saying yes, but his feet are saying no.

Libby picks up the extra tokens. "Do you want to be the hat? Or the boot?"

Aaron wrinkles his forehead. "What boot?"

From the surprised look on his face, I don't think he's ever played Monopoly before.

"Yeah, they're kind of weird. But you pick one of these tokens," I explain. "Libby's always the dog and I'm always the ship, but the rest are up for grabs. Usually, you go around the board and buy any property you can or you want. You have to land on it to buy it. Then when another player lands on that property, they have to pay you rent. We're just giving you some property to catch you up, though."

"And if you land on a railroad, you pay me two hundred dollars!" Libby says. "That's because I own all of them."

From the corner of my eye, I watch Aaron step toward us. "Why's the dog bigger than the ship?" he asks.

"It's a toy ship," Libby says.

"It is not," I say. "It's a real battleship and I'm the captain. You have a giant dog."

"Who would want to be an iron?" Aaron asks, turning the tokens over.

"If you don't like these, we have other games that have people tokens!" Libby offers. "You could be one of the gingerbread boys from Candy Land!"

"I'll be the race car," Aaron says, grabbing up that token.

"Start here on Go. Then you roll when it's your turn." I hand the two dice to Libby so Aaron can watch us go first.

Libby counts up the dots on her roll. "Five!" She stomps her dog down the board to Tennessee Avenue.

"Aaron has that." I show him where the rent is located. "You owe him fourteen dollars, Lib."

I roll and owe him twelve more for landing on Virginia Avenue.

Aaron rolls a five.

"It's my railroad!" Libby sings. "Pay, pay, pay!"

"Is she always like this?" Aaron asks me as he picks up two hundreds.

"Sometimes I'm worse!" Libby grins.

As we play, I'm afraid to let myself be happy — like if I smile or think too much about this moment, I'll ruin it. We're doing something all together, all three of us kids. And it's fun.

When it's my turn, I land on Chance again. I pick up the orange card and shield it from Libby's eyes.

"'Go directly to jail.'" I plop my ship on the corner space. "Good. I'm staying in jail as long as I can. It beats paying rent to Libby."

A shadow falls on the board, and I look up. Dad is standing in the living room doorway, holding a yellow envelope in his hand. "This came for you, Tess."

I hear Aaron catch his breath. I can barely move.

"When you write back, tell the Hamiltons I say hi, okay?" Dad says.

As I take it from him, I look quickly at the front of the envelope. There's only my name and address —

nothing else. Even without a return address, I know it's not from Amy.

"Go, Tess!" Libby shoves the dice onto my leg. "It's your turn."

I throw the dice without even looking.

"You're stuck in jail!" Libby laughs.

Across from me, Aaron stares at my hands as I unfold the letter. There are only two words written inside.

I'll try.

EIGHTEEN

If a bee enters your home,
it's a sign that you'll soon have a visitor.

As the days pass, I make sure that I'm the one who gets the mail every day, just in case Aaron's mother writes again to explain her "I'll try." I'm hoping she'll tell us for sure if she can come to the talent show.

"Has everything been put out?" I ask Mr. Moody.

He smiles. "You must be expecting something important. A letter from Amy, perhaps?"

I nod. It's not completely a lie, because I am expecting a letter from Amy — someday. I wish she'd write, because I have so much to tell her. But it takes two people to be best friends, and lately, I think I'm the only one who still cares.

"I've got a couple piles left to do. Let me see if I have anything for your family." Mr. Moody looks through a stack of letters and bills. "There's some school mail for your mother. And look. The stores are having back-to-school sales already. You'd think they'd let you kids enjoy your summer first, wouldn't you?" Mr. Moody sorts through more mail. I have my eyes peeled for anything yellow in his hands.

"I hear Aaron is playing in the talent show?" he continues. "Mrs. Coombs asked if I'd be Master of Ceremonies again this year."

"Aaron is playing his trumpet. He's playing piano for Libby and Grace's act, too."

Libby couldn't convince me to do an act with her, so she talked Grace into performing a song and dance together. When Libby asked me for a suggestion, I told her bees are lucky (and they're a sign of a visitor coming), so Libby made up a song called "Big, Fat Bees," which is only a little singing and dancing and a whole lot of chasing and buzzing. Aaron's piano accompaniment is the best part of their act.

"I'm glad Aaron is willing to play for us again. It was such a shame what happened at the Fourth of July," Mr. Moody says. "And what about you, Tess? Are you going to perform?"

I shake my head. "I always did something with Amy."

"Well, there's no law against making a change, is there?" He turns over the stack of letters. "Nope, sorry. There's nothing else here for your family, Tess."

"Okay, thanks," I say brightly. "See you later, Mr. Moody."

I wish Aaron's mother could've been a bit more definite. He's excited that she might come to the talent show. I even caught him sliding across the kitchen floor in his socks one afternoon when he thought no one was watching.

But he's short-tempered and prickly about other things. He didn't use to complain to Mom and Dad about anything, but now he's picking battles over the smallest things.

"I need to ask you a few questions," Mom says that night as she's doing some paperwork to register Aaron for school, and he storms off like she asked him to donate his trumpet to Goodwill.

"Well, then, *you* fill this out!" Mom calls after him. She turns to Dad. "What is with him lately?"

Dad strokes his beard. "Remember what they said at training? We'd get a honeymoon period and then he'd feel safe enough to show us another side of him?"

I leave the dishes only half done and head for the attic to talk to him. As I climb the stairs to the second floor, Aaron begins his nightly trumpet practice. But tonight, it's like no music I've ever heard him play before — brassy and wild.

I hate to interrupt him, but I want to tell him to cool it a little before Mom gets suspicious. When he answers my knock, he's holding his trumpet in front of him, his fingers still positioned on the stops. His hair is messy, like he's been running his hand through it.

"I think you should be careful with Mom," I say to him. "Like all mothers, she's got special radar for secrets." As soon as I've said it, I wish I could suck back those careless words. It might hurt him, not having his own mother to complain about. But he doesn't look offended. "That song you played was amazing," I say.

He shrugs. "You can come up to my room and listen if you want."

"Okay." I try not to look too excited — afraid he'll change his mind if he sees how much I want to. In the attic I sit on his bed and wait for him to play, but Aaron looks out the window.

"I want to take a photo of the view here," he says. "Like I did of the mountain at Home Number Two."

"You can look out the window here. You don't need a photo."

He glances to the collage of photos on his dresser. "When I move, I might forget it."

"You won't have to move," I tell him.

"You don't know that," he says plainly. "It happened before. Every time I thought I could count on people — the time came when I was in a car going to another house. I can't keep doing this."

I get off his bed to look at the photos on his bureau. The top photo is a house with a white barn, with blue-gray mountains curving above and behind it. "I miss that mountain," he says.

"Did you know we live on a mountain, too? An island is the top of an underwater mountain."

"It doesn't feel like a mountain, though. Not a real one," he says behind me. "Don't you ever feel closed in, living here?"

I shake my head. "I feel more closed in on the mainland. On an island, you always know where the edge of the earth is. But once you're on the mainland and leave the coast behind, there's only 'middle' running in every direction. I feel lost in all that land."

I blush, because maybe he thinks that's ridiculous. But when I glance at him, he's nodding. "A mountain makes an edge, too," he says.

"Maybe we could go visit that place in your photo sometime," I say. "I bet Dad would take us there when fishing slows down."

"It's pretty in the summer," he says. "And in the fall, but —"

"Is this your band?" I cut him off, in case his next words were gonna be "I won't be here then." I point to the next photo: a group of kids, each holding a musical instrument. I scan the row until I find Aaron's red hair. His smile in the photo looks hopeful and a little shy.

"Yeah. And this is my grandmother." Aaron comes up beside me and gestures to the next picture, an older woman with cat-eye glasses and short, wavy gray hair.

"She looks nice," I say.

"She was." He moves his finger down to the photo in the right-hand corner. "And that's my mom."

She has red hair.

In the photo, his mom's smiling, but it doesn't light her eyes. Everything about her looks a bit out of date — from her makeup to her black dress. She's sitting at an upright piano, but her hands are in her lap, not on the keys. "You look like her," I say.

He nods. "I know."

Inside, I feel like someone is ripping me right down the middle. I want him to stay here with us, but he'll be hurt if his mom disappoints him or doesn't even come.

"I want my song for my mom to be perfect," Aaron says.

"It will be beautiful. You play so well."

"When Mom was a kid, Grandma taught her to play, too," Aaron says. "She told me Mom said that nothing compared to playing piano. Hearing people get all quiet, waiting for you to begin. Then applauding after. Knowing 'I did that.' I feel that way when I play, too. Sometimes when I practice, I imagine Mom's right next to me listening."

"If she comes —"

"She'll come," he says firmly.

"Come where?" a voice asks.

I spin around. Libby's halfway up the stairs, looking at Aaron. How long has she been listening?

"Oh, I forgot to knock!" Libby says. "Good luck you weren't naked, Aaron!" She climbs another stair. "So when's Aaron's mom coming?"

And I know exactly how long she's been listening. Long enough.

NINETEEN

**Cross your heart
to seal a promise.**

One problem with agreeing to keep a secret is that it always starts off feeling like an easy, little decision. But it doesn't stay easy or little. It sits there like one of those jagged ledges hiding under the surface of the ocean at high tide — quietly waiting to rip everything apart if you forget, for even a second, it's there.

Every night after supper, Aaron, Libby, and I walk over to the parish hall to practice for the talent show. Now that it's August, dusk comes a little sooner, and by the time our rehearsal is over, the frogs are trilling and booming in the marsh, and moths dart and dive around us. Every night, I make Libby promise and repromise not to tell about Aaron's mom coming. "Cross your heart and swear not to tell anyone," I say.

Libby draws another X on her chest. "I won't tell."

But my happiness gets punctured a week before the talent show as Libby skips along beside us on the way to practice. "Grace wishes her mom could come to the talent show, too!"

Aaron and I stop short. "What?"

Libby slows down. "It just slipped out. We were talking about who was coming to watch." She chews the side of her lip. "But it's okay. Grace promised not to tell anyone but Jenna."

"Oh, great!" I say. "Why don't we put a sign up on the bulletin board at Phipps's!"

"Jenna won't tell," Libby says.

"I'll make sure of that," I promise Aaron.

"Okay." But he looks concerned.

At the parish hall, Aaron takes his seat at the piano and I sit next to Jenna. While Libby and Grace sing and buzz about on the stage, I'm trying to decide how best to bring up the subject of Aaron's mother. "I'm so glad Grace and Libby have become friends," Jenna says. "It's nice for Grace."

"It's nice for *me*, too, because it keeps Libby busy."

Libby's wearing sunglasses wider than her face. Beside her, Grace looks like she's heading off to Sunday School in a pink-striped dress, little white socks, and black shoes.

"Grace's mom bought her those clothes to wear to church, but Grace won't take them off," Jenna says. "I keep telling her they'll be a mess by Sunday, but she won't listen to me. I don't know why she has to argue over everything."

"She's being a little sister," I say. "You've never had one before, but this is what it's like — some parts are fun and some parts are completely annoying."

Jenna takes a deep breath. "It's hard to think of her as my little sister, though. Because I know she'll probably go back to her mom someday and then we might get another foster child. It won't be for months, though. Her mom has a lot of things she has to do first. This isn't how I thought it would all work out." She blushes. "Not that I don't love Grace."

"Take it from the beginning," Aaron says from the piano bench. "Try to come in together."

I lean close to Jenna's ear and say quietly, "Did Grace tell you Aaron's mom might be coming?"

Jenna nods.

"I hope you'll keep it a secret." I whisper the whole story of the yellow envelopes, Aaron's mom, Gilly Hopkins's story, and Libby's big mouth.

"You don't have to worry about me," Jenna says. "But what if it doesn't work? When Grace sees her mom, she usually gets mad at us afterward. It doesn't make her want to stay with us forever."

"That's different," I say. "Grace is little, and she has a real chance of going back."

"Maybe," Jenna says. "But what if you're wrong?"

"I can't be." My voice sounds certain, but inside, I'm not near as sure.

We sit there watching Libby and Grace flap their arms. "How come you're not doing something for the talent show this year?" Jenna asks me. "You usually do something."

Not without Amy.

"I want to do more than help my dad pass out programs this year. Maybe you and I could do something together?" Jenna looks hopeful. "I'd like to be in the show, but I don't really want to do it by myself." She glances to the stage. "And I definitely don't want to be a bee."

Part of me would like to say yes, but it feels like I'd be cheating on Amy—especially since Amy never really liked Jenna. "I was only gonna watch this year. But okay."

Wait! Did I say that? I swear the part of me that wanted to say yes blurted out "okay" without checking with the "no" side first.

Jenna grins. "Great!"

Oh, glory.

"We could sing an easy song," she says.

Amy and I never did a song, so it isn't exactly like I'm replacing her. And when I pretended to be Lola that night in the parish hall, it was fun. "Um, how about 'Peace Like a River'? I sang that recently and it's not hard, but it's really pretty. And Aaron knows it, so he'd probably say yes to playing it for us."

Jenna smiles. "We'll ask him to play loud. Then we'll sound good, no matter what."

I nod. "Let's ask him to play *really* loud."

"They should call this the no-talent show," a voice says from the back. I whip my head around.

"I was just walking by, and Beast started howling from the terrible noise coming from in here," Eben says.

"Shut up," Aaron says.

"We just came to listen." Eben pats Beast's head, all pretend sweetness. "Can I see your music book, Aaron? I'd like to make a request."

I walk toward him with my fists clenched. "Go away!"

"How about 'All by Myself'?" Eben asks.

"Buzz, buzz!" Libby screams. "Sting them!"

She and Grace jump off the stage. Beast turns to flee, his tail down. Aaron, Jenna, and I laugh as Eben chases after him out the door.

"Grace and Libby might be bees," Jenna says. "But Beast's a chicken."

I grin back, but I can't help the troubled twist in my stomach that Eben came by on purpose. What if he's planning to ruin the talent show, too?

TWENTY

**Never count your catch while
you're fishing, or you won't catch
any more that day.**

Usually, I feel some excitement to see what's in my lobster traps, but as Dad guns the *Tess Libby*'s engine, heading for Sheep Island, I can't stop thinking about the talent show tomorrow.

Beside me, Aaron taps his fingers on the boat rail as if it's a piano.

Off starboard, I watch a small flock of seagulls on the rocks, quarreling over who got what. If they'd only keep quiet, they wouldn't have to share, but gulls can't help bragging about what they've found.

"They sound like a bunch of oboe players," Aaron says. "Really *bad* oboe players."

Dad slows the boat near my first buoy, and a new gull swoops by, dropping a mussel shell on the rocks to break it open. Before he can eat what's inside, another gull grabs it away. The loser throws back his head, giving an earsplitting cry.

Dad leans out to grab my buoy with the gaff.

"Hey, *Tess Libby*, you on?" Uncle Ned's voice comes over the radio. "How's them new traps fishing, Jacob?"

I look over to where Dad and Uncle Ned have set their fake traps as decoys. A bunch of buoys are around them, including one of Eben's. I can't help but smile, knowing he's copycatting a couple of cement blocks.

Dad winks at Aaron and me as he picks up the mic. "I've caught lots today: little ones and big ones."

I touch the blue lettering on the suspenders of my hauling pants. When I first started fishing this spot, I wished: *Please let me have caught some lobsters.*

But I keep catching baby lobsters and one day — the worst-luck day of all — I caught a lobster that was too *big* to be legal. I don't even know how he got himself in the trap.

"Some things should work out but they don't," Dad said yesterday when my trap hauled up with only a couple crabs, a starfish, and a sea urchin inside. "It's not only about what you think or feel is right. It's also knowing when to admit it's time to move on, Tess."

"Not yet." I picked the starfish out of the netting. His tiny pink legs curled against my finger before I dropped him over the rail.

We rebaited the trap, though I could tell Dad thought I was wasting my time.

So today, my wish is:

Please let me have caught some lobsters I can keep.

Wishes are slippery things. You have to be very specific or you can get exactly what you wished for and still end up with nothing. Only when I hear my trap break the surface do I risk a peek.

Dad lets out a long whistle, then clamps his hand over his mouth as if trying to push the whistle back.

I stare, frozen in place. Inside the trap's a brilliant blue lobster! Blues are rare, and this one's the most beautiful color I've ever seen: a gleaming, summer-sky blue.

"Hey, *Tess Libby.*" Uncle Ned's voice comes again over the radio. "Barb wants to know when we can have you all over for supper again? Would tomorrow night suit ya?"

"What are we having for supper, Neddy?" another fisherman asks.

"Barb makes a fine blueberry pie. Think she'd make us one?"

Dad picks up the mic, but he just stands there, holding it.

"None of you is invited!" Uncle Ned snaps. "I'm talking to Jacob."

"It's a public radio," another voice says.

"Ayuh, seems like any invitations ought to be for everyone. Don't you think so, boys?"

Dad clears his throat. "Tess just caught a blue lobster, Ned. Bluest I've ever seen. It doesn't even look real."

"Well, now!" Uncle Ned chuckles. "Guess you've got yourself something special there, Tess. Your daughter's a real Brooks fisherman, Jacob."

I throw Dad a proud look as I band the lobster's crusher claw. "Yes, I am."

Dad sighs and puts the mic down.

"Hey, Tess! I'll pay ya fifty bucks for that lobster," a voice on the radio says.

"I'll give ya sixty!"

"Don't sell it to anyone here, Tess!" Uncle Ned says. "An aquarium somewhere will pay some real money for a blue lobster. I bet Ben Phipps would keep it in the store tank awhile for you, sweetie. I'm sure he'd help you get the best price for it, too."

"Who are you calling 'sweetie,' Ned?" one of the fishermen teases.

"Yeah. I keep telling ya, Ned. We're just *friends*."

"Oh, shut up!" Uncle Ned says.

I fill a bucket with seawater, not even wanting to risk putting this precious, strange thing in with the other lobsters.

"What'll happen to him?" Aaron asks.

"He'll probably live in a big city aquarium where people can admire him." I turn the lobster sideways in my hand to be sure he's blue all over.

Aaron curls his upper lip, disgusted.

"It's better than being *eaten*," I say.

"To live in a strange place and have people watch you all day?"

"He's just a lobster!" I say. "They don't have those kind of feelings."

The weather turns, bringing us in early. I'm glad, because every time I see Aaron looking concerned at the bucket and my lobster, I have to grit my teeth. I can't believe he's trying to make this wonderful gift into a guilty thing.

As we pull up to the wharf, I see a crowd waiting for us. It looks like half the island has gathered near the bait shack.

"Is your lobster very blue?" Libby runs down the wharf, her face glowing with excitement. "Or is he only a teeny bit blue?"

I hold the lobster up to show everyone. Eben turns on his heel and marches away so fast Beast has to run to catch up.

"Amazing!" Reverend Beal says. "A true wonder of nature."

"Have a look, boys," Mr. Morrell says to Matthew and Henry. "You won't see one of those every day!"

"Such a striking color," Mr. Moody adds. "He'll be worth a pretty penny." He grins at me. "Don't spend all that money in one place!"

"I'd like to buy a motor for my skiff with him," I say.

The lobster thrashes his tail, wiggling his spidery legs. Aaron walks by me, bumping my arm. He doesn't say "sorry."

"What color do you suppose this lobster'd be cooked?" Margery Poule asks.

Mr. Moody laughs. "This lobster's worth more than eating."

"He's tired, sweetie," Uncle Ned says. "Best put him back." No longer thrashing, the blue's claws are down, his tail curled under.

When I return the lobster to the bucket, he tries to shoot off backward, but there's nowhere for him to go.

He circles around and around.

TWENTY-ONE

**An itch means
a stranger is coming.**

A Bethsaida talent show is a mixed bag. There's some actual talent like Mrs. Graves, who can sing way up high without screeching (even if you can't understand any of the words). Charlie Lunt plays the cello in the Portland Symphony Orchestra, and he usually brings a few of his musician friends over from the mainland to make a quartet.

And now there's Aaron.

The rest of the show is more funny than good. Last year, the choir sang and then closed their eyes and started snoring when Reverend Beal pretended to give a sermon. Willie Buston always brings his dog, Barty. Last year, they both wore hats and sunglasses and sang "Soul Man." Well, Willie sang — Barty howled. He howled when Mrs. Graves sang up high, too, but that wasn't part of the act.

Then there are always a few performances like Shelby Bowen's baton twirling and Lee Fowler's magic tricks that feel like time standing still. They'd be fine for half a minute or two, but the twirling and abracadabra-ing go on for so long that I usually have time to read my whole program — even the ads in the back.

On the day of the talent show, I dress carefully and put the circle of blue sea glass and all my lucky things in my pocket. If ever there was a day I needed some good luck, it's today.

As I come down the stairs, I feel itchy all over. I hear Mom and another woman's laughter from the kitchen.

Aaron's mother? Heart hammering, I burst into the kitchen.

Mom and Natalie look up from their coffee cups at the table. "Hi, Tess! Look who I invited to the talent show!" Mom says. "I thought it would be a nice surprise for Aaron."

"Oh, glory! I mean, wow. Yes, that's a big surprise."

"I couldn't miss hearing Aaron play." Natalie smiles at Mom. "And Grace is singing, too. Thank you for inviting me. So much of my job is being there for the hard moments in kids' lives. It's great to be invited to something happy."

"I'm delighted you could come," Mom says.

Natalie takes a sip of her coffee. "I'm so pleased to see Aaron joining in and becoming a part of things here. It's exactly what he's needed."

Mom smiles proudly. "We've left the honeymoon stage. He's been showing some rebellion lately. Jacob and I think Aaron trusts us more now to show us his honest feelings."

A fake grin frozen on my face, I back slowly out of the kitchen, unable to break my stare.

Natalie nods. "You're the person who's there, Kate. You're standing in the place of his mom, and that's going to bring up all kinds of mixed feelings for him. He'll push you, because he needs to know if he can count on you and if you're someone who will stay," she adds as I turn for the staircase. "That's always —"

Racing upstairs, I head straight for Libby's room. As soon as the door opens, I push past Libby into her room. "I need you to do something very, very important," I say, pulling her bedroom door closed behind me. "But you'll have to be sneaky."

"Really?" Already dressed in her talent show costume, Libby looks like an evil bee, rubbing her hands together gleefully. "Good."

"Natalie is downstairs. I don't know if she's ever seen Aaron's mom or if his mom's even coming, but I want you and Grace to keep Natalie busy and distracted at the talent show."

Libby nods, her antennae bobbing. "I'll stick to her like pine pitch."

"Perfect," I say. "I'll save some seats in the front row. Make sure Natalie sits there so she doesn't see anyone behind her."

As we head for the stairs, I touch the blue sea glass in my pocket. I think I have everything covered now, but just in case —

Please let this all work out.

It's a tall order, but that's what wishes are for.

TWENTY-TWO

It's good luck to say "break a leg"
before a performance.

As people fill up the rows of folding chairs in the parish hall, Aaron waits on the piano bench at the edge of the stage. Holding the music book upright on his knees, his arms crossed along the top, he stares at the door to outside.

I choose a seat where I can see both the stage and the doorway. It seems like half the island is already here: Uncle Ned, Aunt Barb, Doris Varney, Reverend Beal, Mrs. Coombs. Anna Day even brought her two-week-old new baby, Emma. People stop to smile and say how pretty the baby is. The Morrells are here with Henry and Matthew, and Sam is with the Webbers. Grace and Jenna wave as Natalie walks in with Mom, Dad, and Libby.

"Sit here, Natalie!" Libby says loudly. "Right in the front row with me and Grace. We saved you a seat!"

Natalie smiles. "How nice! Thank you, girls! Are you sure we should sit up front?"

"Yes!" Libby winks at me so big her lip curls up and her bee antennae bobble.

"The front row is the best place to see, because you don't have to look over anyone's hair," Grace adds.

"Hey, Jacob, how's them new traps fishing?" I hear Uncle Ned joke.

"I caught a whole bunch of big ugly ones yesterday," Dad jokes back.

I glance at Aaron, now drumming his fingers on the songbook. His face is toward the crowd, but his eyes are on the door.

I know most of the people coming in, but there are a few strangers. I sneak extra looks at every woman I don't know, but they're all a "wrong" something to be Aaron's mom: wrong age, wrong skin color, wrong size. Maybe his mom couldn't get a ride to the ferry?

Mr. Moody steps to the center of the stage and taps the microphone to see if it works. "Welcome, ladies and gentlemen and —" He glances at Willie Buston and Barty, both wearing Red Sox caps. "Animals!"

"And insects!" Libby yells. "Grace and I are bees!"

People laugh. I glance back to the doorway. Eben

Calder steps in behind Ben Phipps. I look away fast. I don't want Eben to think I was watching for *him*.

I should've made a wish that he wouldn't come.

"Welcome to the Annual Bethsaida Island Talent Show! This year promises to be very entertaining! So, everyone, sit back and enjoy it. And to those of you performing, break a leg!"

"Don't worry," Jenna whispers beside me. "It'll be fine."

But between Eben coming and Aaron's mom maybe not coming, I'm so nervous I can't even enjoy Mrs. Graves's ceiling-high singing or Charlie Lunt's quartet. Shelby Bowen drops her baton four times, and Lee Fowler added a new magic trick this year — but he has to do it twice before it works right. The choir sings while doing a funny exercise routine, and Reverend Beal ends it with a somersault.

"I'll try" is pretty far from a promise. If she doesn't come, Aaron'll be devastated, and he'll want to run away for certain, to make sure she's okay.

When it's Libby and Grace's turn, they flap their arms and buzz up onto the stage. Libby holds the microphone like it's a black ice cream cone, so close to her mouth we hear every breath. "PLEASE DON'T HURT THE BEES!"

Bob Chandler, the soundman, hurriedly turns the volume down on the mic. Anna Day's baby starts crying.

"We eat yellow stuff from trees!" Libby sings.

I told Libby that wasn't technically true, but she seemed to think rhyming mattered more than facts.

"If you give a sneeze, we'll sting you on your knees," Grace sings.

I don't look up until it's done. The old people think it's adorable and clap loudly. Uncle Ned even whistles. Natalie gives Libby and Grace two thumbs-up.

"And now, we have Tess Brooks and Jenna Ross!" Mr. Moody says.

My hands are sweating. Singing is the last thing on earth I feel like doing right now.

"Come on," Jenna whispers, pulling my arm.

Aaron plays an introduction as I step onto the stage. From the audience, Mom and Dad give me big smiles. *Just get this over with.* I swallow hard and lift the microphone. My arm is shaking so much I have to hold on to the mic with both hands.

Jenna starts right in, but the first few words I sing come out really soft. I only let myself look at a few people: Libby swinging her feet under her chair and Mrs. Ellis's head moving in time with the song. I glance quickly to Aaron, but he's concentrating on his playing.

As the second verse comes, I let myself pretend a little. Like when I was Lola wearing a brown scarf and a purple sequined hat. I sing louder.

Ahead, my eye catches a small movement. A red-haired woman is standing at the back. Taking off her sunglasses, she looks around for a seat.

She came.

TWENTY-THREE

It's unlucky to give the last

clap of applause.

"Come on." As the applause dies down, Jenna pulls my sleeve toward the edge of the stage. "We're done!"

My legs feel like they weigh a thousand pounds each. In all the times I imagined Aaron's mother arriving at the talent show, I never imagined I'd feel afraid.

"Now, we're keeping it in the family," Mr. Moody says. "Our final act is Aaron Spinney playing his trumpet for us."

What's gonna happen when he sees her?

"Sit down!" Jenna says between her teeth.

I drop into my seat.

In the audience, my parents smile proudly as Aaron gets up from the piano bench. Mom reaches over to squeeze Dad's hand.

Aaron moves a music stand to the front of the stage. He picks up his trumpet and blows into his mouthpiece to warm it. Stepping his feet apart, he glances at the audience.

I know the second he sees her. He startles, just a little, and then he grins, lifting the trumpet higher.

I shouldn't draw any attention to her, but I have to look. His mother smiles back at Aaron, but her forehead is wrinkled, like she's happy and worried at the same time.

Sharp trumpet notes ring out, filling every corner of the parish hall. Aaron's face changes with the music: his eyebrows lifting with the high notes and coming down with the low ones. He plays the song with a spirit that I almost never hear in his regular speaking voice. Any other day, I'd have gloated over Mrs. Coombs's openmouthed amazement. But today, I barely look at anyone.

He plays as well as I've ever heard him, holding those ending notes long, longer, until it seems like they'll never stop — then a snappy last note, and it's over.

The applause doesn't start immediately — it's like everyone has to catch their breath with him. But when the clapping starts, it's louder than for any other act. His mother stands. She's crying, giving him a standing ovation.

I gasp. *Sit down!*

Heads turn to look. I glance to Natalie. She turns around. Other people get to their feet, too, but I notice Eben stays in his folding chair, his arms crossed over his stomach. He glances at Aaron, then at Aaron's mom, and then to me.

I look away fast.

"Wasn't that wonderful!" Mr. Moody says. "We certainly ended this year's talent show on a high note! I think this was our best year ever. Wouldn't you all agree?" After the applause dies down again, he smiles. "And now Ben Phipps has an announcement!"

Mr. Phipps stands up and looks right at me. "I found a buyer for Tess's lobster. That blue's gonna have to learn to say 'y'all' instead of 'ayuh,' because he'll be heading to an aquarium in Texas!"

People are laughing at his joke, but I can't even smile.

"Congratulations!" Mr. Moody grins at me. "You have lots of talented people at your house, Jacob and Kate!"

Dad nods. "I know it."

"We have a wonderful family," Mom says.

"Aaron's not your family." Eben uncrosses his arms, looking right at Aaron. "He's an orphan."

Dad jumps out of his chair, and Mom doesn't even lift a hand to stop him. But before he can get to Eben, Libby yells out, "Shows what you know, stinky breath!" She points. "*That's* his mother!"

Natalie stands up, and Libby gasps, dropping her hand back to her side. "I'm sorry, Tess! I didn't mean to say it!"

Aaron hurries off the stage toward his mother. Dad turns slowly to look back to me. And I know, sure as certain.

I'm in big trouble.

TWENTY-FOUR

When someone leaves your home,
send him out by the same door he came in.
Otherwise, he'll take your luck away with him.

"I have to trust that my families will act in the best interests of the children in their care." Natalie sits at our kitchen table, her untouched white coffee cup in front of her. "There are reasons for these rules. You can't just decide which ones you'll follow and which ones you'll break."

"Kate and I didn't know about this," Dad says.

Carrie Spinney sits in my chair at our kitchen table. Her long red hair is pulled back straight on each side of her face and held behind with a silver barrette. Up close, she looks pale and older than I expected, like a washed-out version of the person in Aaron's photo. One finger curls through the handle of the cup in front of her, but her eyes are on Aaron. "You played so beautifully today. I had no idea you were such a musician."

Beside her, Aaron looks at the full, untouched glass of water in his hand.

"Remember the toy piano you had? And all your stuffed animals?" Ms. Spinney asks Aaron softly. "I still have them."

His finger traces a droplet down the side of his glass. "Why didn't you ever send them to Grandma's for me?"

"I wanted them for when you came home."

He wipes his finger on his shirt. "Maybe it would've helped me to have them. Did you ever think of that?"

She furrows her brow and glances to Natalie and Mom and then over to Dad and me standing at the counter. "Do you want me to mail them to you now?" She slides her finger out of the cup's handle.

"I don't care about stuffed animals anymore."

"I like stuffed animals." Libby sits across Mom's lap with one arm around her neck. Catching me watching her, Mom gives me the same disappointed-in-you look she gives kids who get a failing grade on a quiz. In her hand she holds the letter I wrote to Aaron's mother.

"You can't imagine how hard it is not to have you home," Ms. Spinney says to Aaron. "Not to be able to just open the back door and yell for you to come in for supper. I don't even know what you might be having for supper."

"Ms. Spinney, this is not helping Aaron," Natalie says, an edge to her voice. "What he needs —"

"We have ocean food a lot," Libby says.

Dad throws me a look, tipping his head toward the screen door. I know he wants me to take Libby outside. But I can't move.

"When can I live with you?" Aaron asks.

Natalie looks mad enough to burst. "This has gone far enough."

"No, it hasn't!" Aaron says. "I need to know if it's ever going to happen."

· Carrie Spinney touches her folded-up sunglasses on her napkin. She doesn't meet his eyes. "Honey, not for a while. Maybe when I have my own —"

"It's never going to happen! Why can't you just *say* that?" he asks. "Grandma said I shouldn't wait for you anymore, because you loved drinking too much to stop. That's why you stopped trying to get me back. I yelled at Grandma for saying that, but it's the truth! You love drinking more than me!"

"That's not true. I love you more than anything." Ms. Spinney shoots Natalie an angry look. "The program they made me do wasn't helping."

"You couldn't have pretended?" Aaron asks.

"That was a hard time for me. It's different now." But seeing her hands quiver, she seems only barely okay. "I just wanted to see you. Someday —"

His eyebrows come down hard. "Don't lie to me!"

"I'm here now, honey, and I'm only here for a day. Do we have to spend it angry?"

"You're my mother, and you don't know anything about me!" he says.

"I know you like applesauce," Ms. Spinney says gently.

"I liked it when I was five!"

"Honey, I don't —"

"I called them! Do you hear me? I called them. I called nine-one-one the day they took me, because I couldn't wake you up! I tried to get you help, and look what happened! They punished *me* for it!" Aaron pushes back his chair and runs for the stairs and his room.

"I shouldn't have come. I didn't want — I don't know how —" Ms. Spinney covers her mouth with her hand, her eyes filling with tears. "He's right. I don't even know what he likes now."

Dad brings her the box of tissues from the top of our refrigerator.

"He likes the trumpet," I say softly. "Especially jazz. And he told me he thinks of you when he plays and imagines you're there to hear him."

Ms. Spinney lifts her head, just enough for her eyes to meet mine above the tissue.

"He also likes mountains and cookie dough ice cream," I continue. "He worries about seals being hungry and whether lobsters are happy or not."

"When we play Monopoly, he picks the race car as his token," Libby adds.

"I need to go," Ms. Spinney says. "This was a mistake."

"No." Mom stands up. "You two need to talk. There are things he needs to say and answers he needs to hear. Let me take you upstairs to him. You have some time before the ferry." She looks at Natalie. "Just for a few minutes?"

Natalie opens her mouth to protest, but then sighs. "I have to come with you."

I wish I could go with them, too, but I know I can't. So I drag myself outside and flop down on the porch steps. Hugging my knees, I lay my head on my arms, feeling low as dirt.

The door opens behind me. From under my arm, I see Dad's sneaker come into view. The top step creaks as he sits down beside me. "What were you thinking?"

Tears come so fast I can't even answer him. I've ruined everything. Now Natalie will probably send Aaron somewhere else and maybe I won't ever see him again. And I may as well pack up all my things with him, because we'll be moving, too.

"Tess, I'm waiting for an answer."

"Aaron wanted to run away," I say, sniffling into my legs. "I heard Mom say that maybe if Aaron could see his mom, he'd give up the perfect idea he had of her. And then maybe he'd be happier to be with us. It worked that way in a book I read." I lift my head, just enough to look at him. "Natalie's pretty upset, huh?"

"Yup," Dad says. "You've got an apology to make there."

I nod. "Will she take him away from us?"

"I don't know. We don't get to decide that," Dad says. "But we'll all go on, whatever comes. Sometimes you have to stop trying to control everything and let life happen the way it's supposed to, Tess. Even if it's not exactly the way you wanted."

I sigh. "But what if it's not even a *little* like you wanted?"

"Then you deal with it and keep going," Dad says. "You and Aaron both have to let go of thinking 'I can only be happy if . . .' and find a way to carry your happiness inside you. We're all more than where we come from, Tess." He puts his arm around me. "I'm not saying it wouldn't be hard to leave here or if Aaron leaves us. But it wouldn't break you. You're stronger than that — whether you realize it or not."

Overhead, a flock of Canada geese flies under the graying clouds. A damp breeze passes, stirring the grass. I cuddle deeper into Dad's side. His shirt smells familiar and snug, of sea and soap and another smell with no name, just a "him" smell.

"We'll never be all Aaron needs, but that's okay," Dad says. "We're *something* to him."

The trumpet music makes us both jump. Sharp and full of life, it's a jazz song. I imagine Aaron's mother sitting upstairs on his bed, listening.

Across the yard, Doris Varney comes out of her front door, carrying her knitting basket. She takes her usual seat on her porch. "Is everything okay?" she yells over to us.

"Not yet," Dad calls back. "But I hope it will be."

"He's such a good kid," Doris says. "And he sure can play!"

Dad lays his head on my hair. "He sure can."

The music is strange and brave and wonderful. I don't know the words or even what the song is called, but I don't care.

It's beautiful, and that's enough.

TWENTY-FIVE

**When beginning a journey,
it's unlucky to look backward.**

After his mother left yesterday, Aaron didn't come out of his room. Dad let him sleep in late the next morning, and even though Aaron agreed to come fishing with us, he barely says a word to Dad and me as we walk down the road to the water together.

He's probably thinking about how Mom and Natalie are having a meeting today to see what needs to happen next. Natalie said she wasn't going to recommend Aaron be moved to another foster home, unless it's what he wanted. But all Aaron would say he wanted was permission to call his mom on the phone sometimes — nothing about us. Mom said she's going to ask for that at the meeting today.

I suppose Dad's right. We're all made up of our bits and pieces. People who love us, places we've lived, and the biggest part of all — who we are inside. I don't know if we've done enough to keep our school open or for how long, but I'm willing to believe that Dad's right about another thing, too. We'll all go on, whatever comes.

"I didn't mean to get so mad at my mom yesterday," Aaron says quietly as we walk. "I thought I would only feel happy to see her and glad she was okay. But when I started talking, it all came out."

Dad puts his hand on Aaron's shoulder. "You needed to say it, and she needed to hear it. You might have a chance to really get to know each other now, without those feelings standing in the way."

"I just wanted to be where I belonged."

I wish I could tell him he belongs with us, but I'm afraid he won't believe me if I just say it. So as Phipps's Gas and Groceries comes into view, I take a deep breath and head for the store porch. "Wait for me. I have something to do. I'll be right back."

"Hey, Tess! Did you forget to set your alarm clock?" Ben says as I come through the door. "You folks are off to a late start this morning."

I go behind the counter and get a bucket. "Mr. Phipps, I'm sorry you went to all that trouble, but I've changed my mind. I'm not sending my blue lobster to Texas."

Mr. Phipps asks plenty of questions, but I just dip

the bucket into the tank to scoop out enough water to make the blue lobster comfortable. Then I push my sleeve way up before I reach down deep.

Dad and Aaron both startle a little to see me hauling a bucket out of the store. "It's my lobster, and I'll do what I want with him," I say firmly, shifting my bucket to hold it in front of me with both hands.

As we near the church, I see Reverend Beal drinking coffee on his front porch steps. Mrs. Coombs looks up from weeding the petunia border.

"Fine morning today!" Dad says.

"Rejoice and be glad in it," Reverend Beal calls back. "Aaron, I want to talk to you. Mrs. Ellis says since we have another pianist on the island now, she'd like you to take over the job as church organist. She said she'd help you get started."

Aaron looks down at the road. "I don't know how long I'm staying."

"As long as *you* want," Dad answers.

"Would you at least think it over, Aaron?" Reverend Beal asks. "We'd pay you, of course. It'd mean Sunday services, Tuesday night choir practice, and the cherub chorus meets on Saturday mornings. Also a few special events here and there."

I have it on the tip of my tongue to tell Reverend Beal no (so Aaron doesn't have to), but when I glance to Aaron, I see something surprising in his eyes. It looks like longing. "Do you *want* to do this?" I whisper.

Aaron lifts one shoulder, like he doesn't care. But his eyes are telling a different story.

"If he says yes, the parish hall piano needs tuning." I call to Reverend Beal. "And you'd need to pay him extra for those special events."

Dad looks surprised, but I tip my chin up, determined.

"Who are you?" Mrs. Coombs sputters at me. "His manager?"

"I'll agree to that," Reverend Beal jumps right in.

"And you will get a haircut!" Mrs. Coombs points her finger at Aaron. "Can't have our organist looking like a hippie. Come by tomorrow so we can fit you for a robe."

"It's Aaron's hair!" I say. "He gets to decide if it gets cut."

Mrs. Coombs's face is turning red. She looks like she might burst a blood vessel right there in the petunia border. "Well, I never saw such —"

"What do you say, Aaron?" Reverend Beal asks. "Do we have a deal?"

Aaron doesn't look at any of us. He just tilts his head, staring off into air beside him. I squeeze the handle of the bucket so hard it hurts.

"Okay," Aaron says.

Reverend Beal smiles. "Thank you."

As we walk away, Mrs. Coombs hurries into the parsonage — to call Mom, no doubt.

"Does this mean you want to stay with us?" I ask Aaron.

He shrugs. "You can keep your school now."

"No, don't stay for that reason." The bucket handle still cuts into my fingers, and I shift hands. "I don't want to move, but I *could*. Stay because you want to be here. Stay because we would miss you. And stay because you can belong in more than one place, and one of your places is with us."

"Listen to her," Dad says. "Because she's right."

Aaron smiles for the first time all morning. He reaches over and takes the bucket from me. "That's too heavy. Let me carry it for you."

As we walk ahead, the bay stretches before us, the sun above the treetops of the far islands. "Look!" I say, pointing ahead. "The Sisters are visiting."

"Catching up on the day's gossip, I guess." Dad smiles. "Ready?"

We pull in our deepest breaths, full of everything before us: pine-covered islands, fishing boats, and seagulls soaring through salt air.

When I can't hold mine one second longer, I let it go. I picture it flowing out of me, down the wharf, and out across the rippling blue-gray waves to the lobster boat moored in the bay.

My heart jumps to see her. The *Tess Libby*, waiting for us.

"Welcome home," I whisper to my lobster.

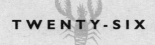

TWENTY-SIX

You make

your own luck.

We've barely started for our first buoy when I tell Dad I want to go to the south end of Sheep Island. As he turns the wheel, I hold my hand over the rail and let sea spray, silky and cold, bead on my wrist and run down my fingers.

On the other side of the boat, Aaron is stuffing bait bags. I imagine him in December seated at the piano in the parish hall, playing carols at our island holiday party. "It Came Upon a Midnight Clear," "We Three Kings," "Away in a Manger" — Mrs. Coombs will want them all. And I'll be singing along in the front row, or maybe I'll even turn the pages for him.

"Why are you smiling?" Aaron asks.

"I was just thinking how Mrs. Coombs will want you to play *Beloved Christmas Carols of Really, Really Old People* on the parish hall piano this December."

"Bah, humbug." He rolls his eyes, but I see the smile he's trying to hide.

Across the water on Bethsaida, two cars drive along the shore road. There are people outside at Amy's old house — must be the summer people who bought it. Maybe I will introduce myself sometime when I walk by.

I promised myself I wouldn't write any more letters to Amy until she wrote to me again, but I'm gonna break that vow when I get home. Maybe she's busy with her new life or maybe thinking about me makes her miss everything she left behind. Whatever her reasons, she's still my friend. I don't want to lose her, even if I write more times than she answers.

I let my eyes move farther up the shoreline to Jenna's house. She's outside with her dog. I lift my arm to wave, though I think it's too far for her to see me.

She waves back and I grin. Maybe Amy and Jenna don't like each other, but that's okay. I like both of them.

As we approach Sheep Island, I take the blue lobster out of the bucket and cut the bands from his claws. He snaps at the air. "Stop right here," I tell Dad.

He slows the boat, and I hold the lobster out to Aaron. "Throw him back."

"What?" Aaron asks. "I can't take him. He's yours."

With my free hand, I clutch my throat, like I'm having an attack. "Oh, Aaron! Don't you know? It's terrible bad luck when someone gives you a blue lobster to refuse it. In fact, it's the worst unlucky thing in the world."

Aaron makes a face. "You're making that up."

"Best not chance it." Dad smiles.

I stand there until Aaron finally reaches for the lobster. Leaning over the rail, he sets him gently on the sea. "Today's your lucky day, blue one."

The lobster stretches out in the sunlit upper inches of water. Flexing his tail, he shoots backward, disappearing down deep.

As Dad puts the boat into gear, I reach into my pocket and pull out two pennies from the year I was born, a teeny plastic lobster, the white quartz heart Amy gave me, the shard of pottery with the sloop painted on it, and my circle of blue sea glass.

Running my fingers around the sea glass's smooth-worn edges one last time, I feel queasy, like I'm about to jump off a cliff without knowing what's waiting at the bottom. I hold my hand over the rail and drop each lucky thing into the ocean so quickly there's barely a splash.

Watching our boat's bubbly wake as we pull away, loss sweeps me — but not a sad loss. More like giving up something I've held on to, and finding it's okay to let it go.

Dad turns us out of the channel, and I stand in the stern, shading my eyes, watching Sheep Island growing smaller behind us. I imagine the blue lobster down there somewhere, climbing over boulders and sunken ship bits.

"I'm glad he's back where he belongs," Aaron says.

"Not really. I caught him over near the Point, not where we let him go."

Aaron's smile falls. "Will he be okay where we left him?"

"Well, he's blue! That's gonna stick out no matter what," I say. "And lobsters are like people: Some take to strangers okay, and others come at each other with their claws wide open. But he's in a good place, and it *can* be a home for him, if he'll let it be."

Aaron looks back toward Sheep Island. "Tess, after the skiff is launched, do you think we could visit Dead Man's Island? I'd like to see that sailor's headstone. Maybe bring him some flowers or something?"

I nod. "It's the first place we'll go."

Dad gives me a proud grin. "Here, Tess. Take over for me," he says, letting go of the wheel.

"What?" I stare at him.

"A fisherman's gotta learn to drive, doesn't she?" he asks. "Or maybe you've changed your mind about wanting—"

"No!" I rush over. Laying my hands on the wheel, a shiver of thrill shoots through me.

"Feels good. Doesn't it?" Dad asks. "Let's practice out to sea where there's nothing to run into."

As I turn the wheel, Uncle Ned's voice comes over the radio. "*Tess Libby*, where are you headed, fool? England?"

Dad pushes the talk button. "Tess is learning to drive the boat, Ned. She wants to join the family business."

"Well, ain't that something!" Uncle Ned says. "But, Tess, if you wanna learn how to be a truly great lobsterman, I could use another sternman. Then you could learn from a *real* fisherman."

"Tess wants to catch lobsters, not seaweed!" Dad snorts.

"Hey, Tess! Watch out you don't hit the lighthouse," another fisherman teases. "It's that big white thing sticking up out of the water."

"Jacob, I hope you're paid up on your boat insurance."

Aaron reaches his hand out for the mic. Dad and I both pause before Dad hands it over. "This is Aaron," he says. "Leave her alone or you'll have to deal with me."

"Oooh," another fisherman says. "Tough words from an *organist.*"

Figures Mrs. Coombs spread that news already! I brace myself for Aaron to be mad, but then he shrugs. "You know," he says slowly. "The organist controls how long the service goes on Sunday. I could keep playing and playing — how many hundreds of hymns do you think are in those hymnals?"

"Now, *that's* a threat," Uncle Ned says. "The reverend goes on longer than enough as it is."

As Aaron puts the mic down, I turn to Dad. "Do you think I could try —"

He nods, reaching over to grip the rail. "Hang on tight, Aaron. Tess is gonna let her loose."

My hands on the wheel, my heart near to bursting, I aim the *Tess Libby*'s bow at the horizon.

And gun it.